LAST
FIRES BURNING

A
Sharyn Howard
Mystery

LAST
FIRES BURNING

•

Joyce and Jim Lavene

AVALON BOOKS
NEW YORK

For the gallant, unsung, rural heroes, the Volunteer Firefighters,
who are called from their beds and families to fight fires
and rescue the unfortunate for no pay and less glory.
Thanks for all your help!

Prologue

It was almost midnight. The acrid smell of smoke from the fires in the Uwharrie Mountains filled the cool air. Sunday nights were quiet in Diamond Springs. Folks tended to go to bed early.

That's why hardly anybody saw the old car roll down the hill from Center Street. Fire shot from the windows and burned through the roof. The car picked up speed as it careened down Main Street past the post office and the hospital. It almost hit one of the well-kept antebellum homes that postured like a queen over her court.

A huge gnarled oak tree stopped it. It was moving fast by the time it hit the tree. Sparks flew up into the highest boughs, burning against the night sky. Flames raced up the tree, igniting the dry branches. Car parts scattered in the street.

Lights came on in the darkness. Sirens flared. Two deputies ran out of the sheriff's office across the street.

"Sheriff's gonna love this," David Matthews declared.

JP Santiago patted his shoulder. "Then I'll let *you* tell her!"

Chapter One

Sheriff Sharyn Howard was at a Halloween fundraiser for the hospital's children's ward. Her Nike tennis shoes were tucked into big red clown's shoes that stuck out about two feet past the bottom of her polka dotted pajamas. Her copper-colored hair was tucked into a wig that was bright orange and stood straight up on her head. White makeup concealed her face behind a big red nose. She looked up at the clock on the wall for the third time in five minutes.

"They say if you keep watching the clock, the time goes by even slower," a smooth voice reminded her.

She continued handing out pledge cards to people as they came in the door. "That's easy for you to say, Nick. You're not dressed up like a clown."

"What do you call this?" Nick Thomopolis, the Montgomery County medical examiner, drew her attention to his perfect black tuxedo and crisp white shirt.

"Go away."

"How about going out for a drink later?"

"Later when? It's almost nine thirty. I have to be at the office at six in the morning."

"Any excuse will do."

She smiled and gave out another card. "It's not an excuse. It's my job."

"Sharyn, you've used every reason possible to avoid going out with me for the past month."

"We watch TV at your place," she objected. "And you've had dinner at my house."

"But we never go out in *public*." He sipped his ginger ale and smiled at her big clown feet. "I'd think you were embarrassed to be seen with me. Except that I know the election committee wants you to keep a low profile on us dating. Well, trying to date anyway."

"Think of it this way," she said. "It keeps our relationship fresh and new. And we've only been trying to date for a few months. We've worked together for the past four years."

"Think of it this way," he replied. "If I get too frustrated, I might grab you and kiss you in the middle of—"

"Sheriff?" Deputy David Matthews frowned when he saw Nick beside her. "Hi Nick."

"Deputy."

"What's wrong, David?" Sharyn stepped out of the flow of traffic from the door.

"A car just rolled down Main Street and hit a tree outside the Hunter's house. It caught that big old oak on fire."

"Is anyone hurt?"

"I don't think so. Fire crew responded. They said no one was in the car. I thought you should know."

Nick watched as David pushed himself closer to Sharyn. The only thing more irritating than keeping quiet about his so-called relationship with Sharyn was David pestering her to go out with *him*. But he had to keep his mouth shut until after the election. "Why didn't you call and tell her?"

David hung his thumbs across his belt and looked important. "I wasn't sure she had her phone with her. And this is official sheriff business. Maybe you should step away for a minute."

Nick laughed at him. He wanted to punch him. "Easy, Romeo. I'm privy to secret sheriff business, remember?"

Sharyn stepped between them. "Give me a break, guys! David, much as I'd like to leave here right now, it doesn't sound like something I need to handle. I'm sure you and JP can do the necessary paperwork between calls."

"Right, Sheriff." David glared at Nick one last time. "Just thought you should be kept informed."

Sharyn's phone vibrated in her jeans' pocket underneath the clown suit. She sighed and took it out. "Sheriff Howard."

"Sheriff, I hate to bother you," Head Deputy Ernie Watkins drawled on the other end. "But I think you need to come down here to this wreck."

"David's right here telling me about it. What's the problem?"

"There's a body in the car after all. JP called me. He said David shut off his phone and he couldn't get in touch with him. I tried to get Nick and couldn't reach him either."

"I'll be right there," she promised. "And I'll bring Nick with me. He's here at the fundraiser too."

"Who was that?" David asked her when she put her phone away.

"Ernie. JP called him because your phone isn't working. Did you turn it off?"

David checked his cell phone. "I didn't do it. It got cut off somehow. Stupid thing."

Sharyn turned to Nick. "Guess you better climb out of that clown suit. You're needed."

He groaned. "Not another investigation. We just closed the McPherson files. I've got finals to give before vacation."

"The McPherson case wasn't that tough. You proved what we already knew: they drowned when their car went off the bridge. Maybe this won't be a murder either." She shrugged as she popped off her clown nose. "But it *is* a dead body that arrived in a burning car."

"I thought you said no one was in the car?" Nick cornered David.

David grinned at him. "I said the fire fighters said there wasn't a body. You know they can't half do their job!"

Sharyn ignored them both and went to explain to the committee chair that she had to leave.

"Sorry to see you go." Commissioner Charlie Sommers

shook her hand. "Is there an emergency? I thought I heard sirens earlier."

"Hopefully nothing serious," she answered blandly. "Good luck with the fundraiser."

"Thanks, Sheriff. We've already done pretty well, thanks to your help." He shook hands with David and Nick also. Election day was only a week away.

"Charlie Sommers keeps on pumping, doesn't he?" David said as they were leaving the hospital. "I mean his daughter is murdered. He has to commit his wife. Still he heads the hospital board and runs for re-election for the county commission."

"Some people don't give up." Sharyn wished he'd keep his voice down. She was glad when they reached the parking lot. She stopped to take off her clown shoes so they wouldn't get dirty since she had rented them.

David was immediately at her side. He took her hand as she reached out to rest it against the hospital's brick wall for support.

"Thanks, David." It didn't take any imagination for her to feel Nick's glare laser through David's head. She knew he had a problem with David.

"No problem, Sharyn."

"I drove down here." She was sandwiched between them as they reached her car. Not in a hurry to continue fending off David and deflecting Nick, she said, "I'll meet you both down at the office."

David stared at Nick who frowned at Sharyn.

"I could ride with you," David volunteered first. "I didn't drive down."

Nick shook his head and walked away.

"David, you and I are going to have a talk," she told him when they were alone. "Get in."

The hospital was only five minutes from the sheriff's office. There wasn't time to explain to David that she didn't want his romantic attention. She decided to put it off until after she saw what happened at the wreck scene. Not that she didn't say it before. Many times before. She thought it would pass by now. His attention span where women were concerned was usually about three weeks. It was already three, long months.

A crowd was gathering on the street beside the old tree. She parked her Jeep at the edge of the yellow tape Ernie and JP had strung to keep back the spectators. David jumped out and ran around to her side to open the door for her. She stopped him by pushing it open and climbing out by herself. His hurt puppy-dog look was almost enough to make her laugh out loud. Before he decided that he was in love with her, they had argued about everything. She almost had to suspend him on a few occasions.

"Sheriff." Ernie Watkins held up the police tape for her. "Nice outfit."

"Thanks. Let's not mention it again, huh? What happened?"

"Let's confab over here with Chief Wallace. David, give JP a hand with crowd control, son." He walked beside her. "I see the boy's still all over you."

Sharyn had removed her wig in the Jeep. She wiped away most of the white makeup as they walked through the heavy smoke and debris. "Honestly, I liked him better when he disagreed with everything I said and thought he should be sheriff."

Ernie laughed. "You could do worse, you know? David's your age. He's in law enforcement. Maybe you should forget about Nick and try going out with him. Try having some fun once in a while. You know your daddy did lots of other things besides being sheriff."

She knew he was teasing. "My dad fished, Ernie. He didn't date deputies for recreation! Besides, I have enough trouble with Nick."

His long pointed nose twitched with suppressed laughter. "Of course you do. That's why I worked so hard getting the two of you together. I wanted you to be as happy as me and Annie."

"Can we talk about dead bodies or something else more pleasant?"

They finally maneuvered their way through the burnt branches and water puddles to find Fire Chief Dennis Wallace. He was dressed in a bright yellow jacket and wore a Diamond Spring's high school cap. The old fire chief retired earlier that month after being overcome by smoke in the mountains.

"Sheriff," Dennis greeted her, taking her hand in a hearty clasp. "Nice outfit."

"I'll cut you some slack on that remark since you're new, Chief," she answered. "What can you tell me so far?"

Dennis Wallace brought them closer to the burnt car. "It was on fire before it hit the tree. We've had a few reports from witnesses who saw it. I think your deputy said he had a few phone calls after the impact."

"Good of them to call after the fact," Ernie said with a lopsided grin.

"We had a few too, Chief." A woman joined them wearing a hazard suit.

"Oh Sheriff, this is my assistant, Melinda Hays," the chief introduced them.

"Hi Melinda." Sharyn shook her gloved hand. "How's it going? Melinda and I graduated high school in the same class."

"That's right. I'm doing well. How are you, Sheriff?" Melinda asked with a smile on her sooty face.

"Pretty good," Sharyn responded. "Wishing the election was over and done with."

"Yeah. Well, you got my vote anyway. I think you've done a good job."

"Thanks, Melinda."

"If you ladies are finished chatting?" Chief Wallace interrupted. "As I was saying, the car was on fire. Your deputy first on the scene thinks it's the wreck that was tagged up on Center Street."

Ernie looked at his notebook. "JP said it was scheduled to be picked up tomorrow morning. Black '76 Ford LTD."

"We think it probably caught on fire when the owner

tried to move it," the chief explained. "We'll know more when we do some work on it."

Ernie whistled through his teeth. "Pretty good impact."

"Almost knocked the tree over," the chief remarked, showing them the black indentation in what was left of the tree.

"Who did the car belong to, Ernie?" Sharyn asked.

"It was abandoned. They didn't find a registration or tag for it when they decided to tow it. We'll have to look it up by the serial number on the engine."

"Didn't someone do that before this happened?" Dennis questioned. "Don't you guys get paid for that kind of stuff?"

Ernie glanced up at him. "We don't check out the serial number on every abandoned car, Chief. If a car looks like it was used in a crime, that would be different. Otherwise, that might be a waste of all that money you're paying us."

"Good luck finding it now." The chief showed them the engine. It was black from the fire and dented from being pushed back into the front seat of the car.

"Isn't that *your* job, Chief? Part of the fire department investigation?" Sharyn coughed a little. Her throat was raw. The stench of burned tree and car was almost overpowering.

"Are you making it my job, Sheriff?"

"Yes, I think I am. I heard about your new arson team. Sounds like a good job for them.

Dennis cleared his throat. "We don't *officially* have a new arson unit yet."

"But I'm sure you have *someone* who can do the job," Sharyn persisted.

"You're aware that we've been fighting the fires in the mountains for a month, right?"

Sharyn smiled. "You know the sheriff's department has been there beside you, right?"

The chief shrugged, giving in. "Okay. You got it, Sheriff."

"Thanks, Chief."

"Now what about a body being in the car?" Sharyn walked around to the driver's side.

"Actually, it's in the backseat," Melinda told her. "That's why we didn't see it right away. You don't expect to find a body in the back when there isn't one in the front."

"The back seat?" Ernie quipped. "No wonder he hit the tree."

"That kind of shoots the engine catching fire when the driver started the car theory, doesn't it?" Sharyn waited to look in the car while two firemen removed the charred back door.

"The impact could've thrown him back there." Dennis wiped the sooty sweat from his forehead on his jacket sleeve.

"Impact tends to throw a person forward from the driver's seat," Ernie pointed out. "Like through the windshield."

Sharyn moved closer to the backseat. It was a blackened hole exposed by taking off the door. Stretched out on the seat was what was left of a human body. She could make out the arms thrown above the head and legs sprawled wide. The torso was a burnt cavity.

The smell was awful. Sharyn put her hand to her face to block the smell as she observed the area. Bits of a plaid jacket and green pants were melted on the bones.

Nick walked up behind the group with his team of college students. The group was all he could afford to hire on the limited budget restrictions that the county allowed him. They came from his pathology class. Helping the Montgomery County coroner carried two extra credits. "Somebody forget to put out a cigarette?"

"Nick." Chief Wallace took his hand. "Glad you're here. I was afraid the sheriff was going to ask me to do the autopsy next."

"I have that affect on people." Nick shrugged as he put on his gloves. "It makes me the life of any party."

Sharyn moved aside as he joined them. "Lucky thing the car didn't explode."

"Gas tank position," Melinda told her.

"The body was protected by the seats folding over it," Nick added.

Melinda smiled at him. "That's what I thought too, Dr. Thomopolis."

"Call me Nick. And you are?"

"Melinda Hays. I'm the chief's new assistant."

"Nice to meet you." Nick knelt down on the ground and looked at the backseat and the corpse. "I can tell you that this was a man. Approximately 5'10 or 11."

"I saw that," Sharyn mentioned.

"I'm sure you did, Sheriff," he commended wryly.

Ernie groaned. "Are we back to that? I thought you two were getting along better."

Nick didn't respond as he turned back to the corpse. "There's not enough skin left for fingerprints. We'll have to do dental records. Maybe DNA if we have something to compare it too. Do we think this is the owner of the car?"

"We don't know yet," Ernie told him. "We should have that for you in the morning."

"It would be someplace to start." Nick sniffed. "What's that smell?"

"In all this stench, who can tell?" Sharyn moved her hand from her nose and sniffed. There *was* a distinct aroma beyond the odor of charred flesh, car, and tree.

Ernie popped his head down close to the seat. "I know that smell. Whiskey. High test. My uncle used to run it out through Asheville when I was a kid."

Nick nodded. "I'm not an arson expert but it looks to me like the body is burned beyond the interiors around him. I should be able to test the fragments of the clothes. I think the man might have been set on fire, possibly with whiskey, then the rest of the car caught on fire from him."

"You're as close to an arson expert as this town has," Chief Wallace told him. "Melinda is starting school in January but we don't have an arson team yet. As I was telling the sheriff."

"You're going to be an arson investigator?" Nick questioned Melinda with a grin. "That makes us cousins, I think."

"Kin," she corrected him. "I can tell you aren't from down here, Nick!"

Sharyn was getting annoyed. There was no reason to get annoyed. Except that Nick was purposely flirting with Melinda to annoy her. He was doing it to get back at her for David. It was stupid and childish. She sighed. And it was working.

Nick finished up and removed his gloves. "That's about all I can tell you for now. Chief, if you could do your thing on the car, maybe Melinda and I could coordinate our efforts. I'll take the body and let her know what we find."

"Thanks, Nick. We'll have the car picked up."

"Maybe both of you could keep the sheriff's office informed of any progress?" Sharyn asked.

"Of course," Nick answered smoothly. "Otherwise, they don't pay me."

Sharyn managed to slide past Nick and Melinda. "Hi Megan. Keith."

"Nice outfit, Sheriff." Megan popped her gum. Her dyed black hair, black clothes and heavily made up eyes were appropriate for the situation. She looked like an undertaker.

"Thanks."

"Hi Sheriff." Keith Reynolds approached her.

Sharyn expected Keith to ask about her sister, Kristie. He did every time they met since they broke up last spring. But she guessed he finally got tired of asking. She saw him talking to Megan with his head close to hers. It was just as well. Kristie was still on the road to recovery after a near breakdown following an attempt on her life. She wasn't fit for any relationship yet.

Reporters were waiting outside the tape line. So was Roy Tarnower, Sharyn's rival in the coming election for sheriff. He always turned up where there was trouble. It was a chance to make her look bad. So far, it was working. She'd gained in the polls in the past few months but he was still ahead. If things didn't change around in the next week, it was likely he'd win the election. Until then, she had a job to do.

"Sheriff? What happened? Isn't there any way to keep Diamond Springs safe from crime anymore?" Roy yelled through the crowd.

The reporters wrote down his words like he was Aristotle. They were having a feast on the history between them.

Roy was sheriff of Diamond Springs once. For one term between Sharyn's grandfather and her father. He tried to have her removed when she took office after her father was murdered. He was supported by former District Attorney Jack Winter who was running for state senator. There was no love lost between Jack and Sharyn. There was bad blood all the way around. The press loved it.

"No one said this was a crime, Mr. Tarnower," she reminded him. "Preliminary reports verify that a man's body was found in the backseat of the car. We don't know his identity yet. It could be foul play or it could be careless smoking habits. We'll release more information when we have it."

"How would you handle this differently if you were sheriff, Mr. Tarnower?" Foster Odom asked looking particularly greasy in the smoky light. He was a reporter with The Diamond Springs Gazette. They were supporting Tarnower for office.

"If I were sheriff," Tarnower reminisced as the crowd turned to him, "these types of things wouldn't go on every day in Diamond Springs. This used to be a peaceful town. And—"

"And if I'm elected, Diamond Springs will go back to being a peaceful town," Ernie muttered under his breath for Sharyn's ears only as they left the scene. "Yeah, yeah, yeah. We heard that tune, old son."

"He's got a point." Sharyn walked with him across the street to the sheriff's office. "When I was growing up, Diamond Springs *was* different."

"But it'd be different no matter who was sheriff," Ernie

responded. "Times change. People change. Him being sheriff won't make things go back the way they were. Why can't people see that?"

Sharyn glanced at him, surprised by his outburst. Ernie usually didn't get involved in politics.

"Sorry." He pulled at his hat. "Just burns me up that he might win this election. I'm not ready to retire yet."

Foster Odom ran up and nudged his way between Sharyn and Ernie. "By the way, sheriff." His photographer snapped a picture of her before they left. "Nice outfit."

Sharyn took a deep breath and counted to twenty. She was able to count to ten and calm down before the whole election procedure started. It didn't work anymore. She needed more time to cool down.

"No doubt that will be on the front page tomorrow." Ernie made blocks with his hands to resemble headlines. "The sheriff is a clown. We need Roy Tarnower."

"I'm sure they'll be more creative than that," Sharyn said, laughing as they entered the sheriff's office. "Do you want your sheriff to act like a clown? If not, then vote for Roy. He won't let you down."

"That's good, sheriff," Deputy JP Santiago remarked as they came up to the front desk.

"Honey, you could be a poet," Marvella Honeycutt added with a wave of her hand. Marvella had worked as the janitor there for the past two years while she put herself through college. "But change those clothes! You might as well give that evil man the vote!"

"I was at a benefit for the children's wing at the hospital," Sharyn explained to everyone. "We raised over thirty thousand dollars before I left. I think that's worth looking stupid."

"Nothin's worth looking stupid, Sheriff," Marvella informed her. "How you look is who you are."

"I have the messages from the people who saw the car," Deputy JP Santiago interrupted, handing her the messages all carefully scrolled in his very nice penmanship.

"Thanks. How's the baby doing?"

"Fine, thanks to Marvella," JP told her. "She gave me a cure for colic and now he sleeps every night."

"Marvella knows it all," Ernie said, taking off his jacket.

"That's right, honey," the sassy African-American janitor told him. "And you will miss me when I'm gone come January. How will you get along without me?"

"I reckon we'll find a way," Ernie teased her. "We might have to take our babies to the doctor and find someone who can tell the sheriff how to dress."

Sharyn turned to him. "You don't have to stay. Go on home. JP and David can handle it. Their shift just started. I know Annie doesn't like you out this late."

"Annie understands that I have to be here sometimes," he assured her. "Besides, you're staying."

Sharyn sighed. "Yes."

"Then so am I. Where's the coffee?"

"Deputy Santiago and I made a fresh pot a few minutes ago," Marvella told him. "I added my own special touch."

"Windex?" Ernie asked with a smirk on his craggy face.

"Do you think this is another murder?" JP asked Sharyn, worried furrows in his brow.

"We've already had our share this year." She poured out some of their special brew. "I hope not."

"Looks like it could be an accident," Ernie answered. "No reason to think more until something else turns up."

Sharyn agreed. "In the meantime, let's check out that car. It's our only lead until we hear something from Nick or the chief."

David came running into the office. "Chief Wallace says they can't hold the fire line on Diamond Mountain. He says they're going to have to run and re-trench, hope they can hold it somewhere else."

"I hate to do it, Ernie, but let's call in Ed, Joe and Cari. Get Trudy in here and have her call in all the deputized citizens and volunteers. David, you and JP take my Jeep up there. Ernie and I will take over patrol until this clears up."

David came closer to her. "I can handle this, Sharyn. But

it could be dangerous. Isn't there something you'd like to say to me before I go?"

That was it. She grabbed him by the arm and hauled him into her office. She slammed the door closed behind them. "David, I've tried to tell you nicely, even politely, a dozen times that you and I aren't going to date or whatever you have in mind for us. We aren't going to be a couple."

"Because of you being sheriff?"

"No! Because you and I would never work out. You don't really love me. I don't love you. You're a good deputy. We've seen some rough times together but we've worked through them. Don't make me suspend you over this."

David hung his head. A swath of brown hair fell forward on his face. He looked up at her through it. "I just want to be with you, Sharyn. To protect you. To share your life."

She ground her teeth. What would it take to convince him? A light popped on inside her head. Suddenly it was clear to her. "You know that Nick and I are dating. And it's pretty serious. That's why it won't work between us."

His face changed. "If you would've told me it was *serious* between you—"

"I just did."

He stared hard at her then stormed out of her office.

Sharyn slumped down at her desk.

"You finally found a way to make him stop fawning all over you?" Ernie sat opposite her at the big wooden desk that had once belonged to her father.

"Yeah. I told him Nick and I are too serious for me to fool around with him."

Ernie pushed the tiny sprig of hair back on his head. "Good idea. I'm gonna see if I can find out something about that car. You want to take calls?"

"Sure. Anything to stop talking about my love life."

"What love life? Oh, that's right. You and Nick *do* watch some TV together."

Sharyn ignored him. She went to change into her tan and brown sheriff's department uniform. She lost about ten pounds working in the mountains during the fires. It still didn't help the way the uniform sat on her body. She clipped on her badge and her grandfather's service revolver. She was sheriff of Diamond Springs until the end of the year anyway. Even if she lost the election, transition wouldn't take until January 1st.

A call came in about ten minutes later. Sparks from the fires on Diamond Mountain were showering a barn. The farmer was worried that he might lose everything. Sharyn called the fire department but all units were on the mountain trying to contain the fire. She told Ernie she was going out to see what she could do.

It was frightening to look up and see the top of the mountain on fire. It towered over Diamond Springs like a hunchback giant. The Uwharries were drier than they'd been in over a hundred years. Only a few inches of water fell in the summer. They said it was a lightning strike that started the current fire. They were battling small brush fires all autumn. The area was experiencing terrible electrical storms at the same time that the trees and ground were powder dry. It wasn't a good combination.

Smoke from the constant small fires filtered down through the county. Since July, you couldn't walk outside without smelling it. The battle weary faces of the firemen and volunteers made the news every night. The four-year drought whittled down the water in the lake to dangerous levels too. Even with Diamond Lake in the heart of the city, no one was sure they could save the town. If a big fire started on the mountain and the wind blew it their way, Diamond Springs would be in trouble.

It made everyone restless and edgy. The sheriff's office answered more domestic disturbance calls than normal in the past few months. There were more problems with neighbors fighting over stupid little things. One man knocked another in the head with a rake because his leaves kept blowing into his yard. It was crazy and scary.

Wild animals were a real problem too. Bears, deer, raccoons, and skunks were chased down the mountain by the heat and smoke. They picked up three bears in the last month in the city limits. They rarely saw that many in a year. Animal control fell in the sheriff's jurisdiction in Montgomery County. Budget cuts last year forced out the animal control officers.

Otis Fielding was standing beside the dark silhouette of his barn, staring at the sparks flying off the mountain. "This don't look good, Sheriff."

"I know. Let's get out your hose and wet everything down, Otis. Maybe they'll get it stopped before it gets any worse down here."

There wasn't much pressure to the hose. Not enough to reach the top of the barn, the most vulnerable point. Water supplies dwindled as the water table dropped. They would have to make do.

Sharyn heard the frightened bellowing of the cows in the old barn. Chickens flapped into the yard. The night was lit up by the terrible red glow.

"My sons are on their way from Albemarle. I don't know if they're gonna make it in time."

She looked at the eighty-four-year-old man who could barely walk. Someone was going to have to go up on that barn to wet it down. He wasn't able to climb up there. And with his sons coming from Albemarle . . . "I'll start up. Pull out the hose as far as you can."

Otis did as she asked. There were rough wooden slats that ran up the side of the barn creating a crude ladder to reach the roof. Sharyn started up. She could see the terrified animals through the chinks in the old wood. Otis handed her the hose. She needed both her hands to climb up so she tied it loosely around her waist.

The fire on the mountain was coming steadily closer. Pinpricks of ash and burning debris were floating down all around her. It wouldn't take long to ignite the old barn. The scorching summer heat and no rain made it tinder for the fire.

Moving slowly and carefully, she reached the top. Some

spots were already on fire. Like destructive insects, the sparks kept falling, beginning to devour the roof. She unwrapped the hose from her waist. "Turn on the water, Otis!"

Chapter Two

Water didn't exactly shoot out of the hose. It trickled a little then squeezed out a little more until it was a fine spray. Sharyn kept spraying the roof until all of the tiny fire demons were gone. Water dripped from the eaves. The sparks still fell all around her. Most became a gray ash that covered the trees and the roof. Probably her too. She didn't have time to think about it. She was more worried about falling through the paper-thin roof and having a startled cow kick her.

Two hours later, Otis Fielding's sons arrived together in a beat-up truck. The worst of the fire on the mountain was over. Reports coming in on her radio told Sharyn that the fire fighters were successful in re-directing the fire. Diamond Springs was safe again for a while.

"Thanks, Sheriff." Tad Fielding shook her hand.

"Sure thing." The muscles in her hand twitched from holding the water hose one way for so long. "I'm glad you boys could get here. The ash might be enough to crush that roof."

"Yeah, Daddy needs a new one," Tad Fielding agreed, gazing up at the roof of the barn.

She dusted off her uniform. Heavy gray ash flew everywhere. She tried to get most of it out of her hair before she got back in the patrol car. It was still dark when she left the Fielding farm. The top of Diamond Mountain was smoking but the orange fires were gone. Exhausted, she drove back to the office.

Charlie was already there in the back lot. "Heard the call for everyone to come in. Figured you could use the help."

She smiled at him. "Thanks, Charlie."

"Sure thing, Sheriff. Don't know what the dogs would do without me anyway."

"I don't know what any of us would do without you." She waved to him and parked her car. David and JP were back with her Jeep. It was covered in wet ash but otherwise unharmed. She finally forced her legs to get her out of the car and walk into the office.

There were volunteers everywhere. Reports came in regularly from the fire fighters still on the mountain. The fire wasn't out. They managed to shift it but it still raged on the other side. Sharyn wondered why JP and David were back so soon.

"Chief Wallace got some fresh blood from the Stanley County rescue squads," Ernie answered her unspoken question. "We had a big wreck on the Interstate. Casualties and two dead. Highway Patrol needed our help. I sent JP and David out there."

"Stop doing that, Ernie," Sharyn said irritably. "At least let me ask the question before you answer it."

His mustache twitched. "Sheriff, you need a shower and a change of clothes followed by some strong coffee. You're a mess."

"Thanks. I saved Otis Fielding's barn."

"Those two boys of his are worthless," Ernie observed.

She didn't disagree. "Where's Ed, Joe, and Cari?"

"I sent them home. I figured we didn't need them now but we'll need them later this morning. Trudy came in for a while then she left too. Plenty of volunteers who can sleep late tomorrow."

"That's fine. I'm going to catch that shower and change clothes. I don't know about the coffee."

She realized as she stripped off her uniform that sparks burned a few places on her shoulders and back. Her hair was matted and gray with ash. Her skin felt coated in it. So did her mouth and throat. She showered quickly, glad that the sparks stopped at her uniform. A mental picture with her hair on fire made her lips turn up into a smile. It was a common analogy for people to use for her penny bright hair.

Showered and dressed in a new uniform, she went back into the office and grabbed a Coke from the fridge. It was almost 6 A.M. time for her shift to begin. It was going to be a long, caffeine-fed day.

The television was on with scenes of the fires on Diamond Mountain. In between was a commercial with her face on it. It countered Roy Tarnower's complaint about her lack of experience. Pictures flashed of her doing her job. They were staged, of course. A deep voice said, *"Sheriff Sharyn Howard: Not just experience. The right experience."*

"I love that commercial." Ernie stopped to watch beside her.

Sharyn countered. "Roy's right on that point. He has a lot more experience than me. I've been sheriff for four years. He was sheriff for four years and a deputy for eight."

"That's what I like about the commercial," he argued. "You might not have as much experience but what you've got really counts."

Sharyn's ad was followed immediately by an ad for Jack Winter. He quit his job as DA for Diamond Springs over the summer when Caison Talbot's fortunes changed. Caison was district senator for twelve years. He was accused of murder in a move that some people blamed on the DA's office. Winter swooped in like a vulture to run for the senator's job.

"Jack Winter: Prosecutor. Not politician."

"I hate that one," Ernie said. "I can't believe people will vote for that man."

"He's ahead in the polls."

"So is Roy. But I know you're gonna win."

"How?"

He patted his flat stomach. "My gut. I know it in my gut. It's never wrong."

Sharyn looked at his sparse, wiry frame. "Great. Does your gut tell you who's going to win the South Carolina lottery too? If it does, let's buy a ticket."

He wagged a finger at her. "You're mocking me."

She laughed. "Not really. I know you want me to win. I want to win too. I don't know anything else I can do besides doing my job."

"That's all you need to do. People know you do a good job, Sheriff. They'll vote the right way."

She sat down behind her desk. "Anything on that car yet?"

"Nope. No car matching the description has been reported stolen. I didn't think it was likely but I checked. With the fire fighters up on the mountain, I don't know how long it'll take to check that serial number."

Her phone rang. Ernie left her to answer a call in the main office. "Sheriff Howard."

"Good morning." Nick's voice rasped over the line.

"Good morning. Have you been up all night too?"

"Yeah. How else will I win the medical examiner of the year award for Montgomery County?"

"I'd laugh but I'm too tired."

"I know you've been up all night. I saw exclusive footage of you fighting the fire at somebody's farm. You looked like a Valkyrie standing up on that roof."

"Really?" She played with the pens and pencils on her desk. "I didn't know there were reporters there."

"They've been around so much lately, you've become immune to them."

"Like becoming immune to you?"

Nick sighed deeply. "Don't press your luck, Sheriff."

"Just call me Nick," she mimicked his voice when he was speaking to Melinda.

"You were jealous!"

"Not unless jealousy is accompanied by nausea."

"You were jealous. Admit it!"

She broke a pencil point on her desk. "Get to the point, Nick."

"The point is that you were jealous because I was talking to that future arson investigator."

"I'm working," she replied calmly. "If you only called to harass me, I'm going to hang up."

"Meet me for breakfast. People will think we're working. It's not as insidious as dinner."

"Okay," she agreed. "I'll be at the diner in ten minutes."

True to her word, Sharyn was at the diner a block away in ten minutes. Ernie was on one side of her and Charlie, the impound officer, was on the other.

"Coward," Nick whispered as she passed him to scoot into the red and brown plastic booth.

"I'm starved." Ernie rubbed his hands together. "I think I'll have the pancakes *and* the eggs this morning."

"Not me," Charlie said, looking at the menu. "Eggs give me gas."

Nick glared at Sharyn who sat beside him. She smiled serenely back at him.

"So, what's up?" Ernie asked Nick after they ordered. "Anything yet on that body?"

"Not yet," Nick answered. "I've taken some tissue and hair samples. I can tell you that he was wearing a red plaid flannel jacket and green twill work pants. We found fried Converse on his feet."

"Converse?" Charlie's wizened face wrinkled into a query. "He must'a had some money then. Those things are pricey."

"Could be," Ernie agreed. "But they also give them out at the homeless shelter from time to time."

"It was a cold night," Sharyn considered. "It's not impossible to imagine that a homeless man would decide to spend the night in the car."

"And what?" Nick questioned as their breakfasts arrived. "He douses himself with whiskey then lights himself on fire? Then sets the car rolling down the street?"

"Stranger things have happened," Ernie said, tucking into his eggs. "Pass the ketchup, Sheriff."

She passed the bottle, munching thoughtfully on her egg sandwich. "Maybe it didn't happen the way you're saying, Nick. But he could've been drinking, spilled some and lit a cigarette. People burn themselves to death every year that way. He could've kicked the car into gear thrashing around trying to stop the fire."

"Good theory," Charlie commended.

Nick shook his head. The sunlight picked out the strands of gray in his black hair. "I have some other news. Melinda stopped by and told me that she got the serial number from the car."

"Stopped by?" Sharyn lifted her cinnamon colored eyebrow. "That was convenient."

Nick grinned at her. Ernie and Charlie didn't look up from their food.

"Anyway, here's the serial number." He gave it to her, making sure their fingers touched as he did it.

She took it quickly and shoved it into her pocket. "Thanks."

"Don't mention it. I have classes this morning but I should be able to work on the body the rest of the day. He's got a lot of fillings in his teeth. Even if we can't find dental records, we might be able to tell something from that."

"Yeah, I read about that." Ernie pointed with his fork. "Something about the fillings put in by military dentists not being made of the same stuff civilian dentists use?"

"Yeah. I can check for that and I'll do a scan to check for broken bones and other anomalies."

"Good." Sharyn finished a few bites of her sandwich and swallowed the last of her coffee. "I have to get back to the office."

"Sheriff!" Foster Odom stopped at their table. He pulled out his tape recorder and signaled his photographer. "Hard at work on that new murder case, huh?"

The photographer snapped photos of them and their empty breakfast plates.

"Mr. Odom, everyone eats breakfast," she told him plainly. "Why don't you go and dig up something more interesting for the paper."

"I have something more interesting." Ernie got to his feet. "Is that your van out there, sir? If so, you're in direct violation of the fire code by parking in the fire lane."

Odom laughed and signaled the photographer to stop. "Harassing me won't help your boss keep her job, Deputy."

Ernie sniffed and took out his citation book. "Can't hurt either, sir. I'll need to see your registration, please. Is that a bald spot I see on that rear tire?"

The reporter was furious but he knew when to back off. "I'm going. Good luck with that murder case, Sheriff."

"If you call it that in the paper," Sharyn warned, "I'll ask Jimmie Dalton for a retraction. Things are bad enough right now. We don't need you printing things that aren't true."

Odom smiled nastily. "Desperate times, huh, Sheriff? It's going to be my pleasure to dance at your concession speech."

Nick stood up next to the two men. Charlie stood up too, for good measure.

Odom took a step back and his photographer got behind him. "Always plenty of people to defend you, Sheriff. I'll see you later."

"All of you can stop glaring now." Sharyn got up and slid out of the booth. "He's just an annoyance, you know."

Ernie disagreed. "He's a pain in the—"

"Never mind!" She headed for the door. "Thanks for breakfast, Nick. I'm late for the county commission meeting, as usual. Ernie, will you get started on—"

"I'll have it by the time you get back," he promised.

She frowned and left them there.

Ernie laughed. "She don't like it when I finish her sentences or know what she's gonna say before she says it."

"Margery's like that with me. It's nice," Charlie observed. " 'Course, you and the sheriff aren't married."

"Nope and not likely to be," Ernie assured him. "We think a lot alike is all. I'm leaving that other part to Nick. He might just wear her down."

"Like pouring water on a diamond?" Nick suggested with a smile.

"Cheer up, old son." Ernie patted him on his back. "The election will be over soon. You'll be able to go out to dinner without it being a work situation."

"Not soon enough for me."

"I gotta get back to work. Thanks for breakfast, Nick." Ernie left him with the check.

Charlie smiled. "Yeah, thanks, Nick."

"Sure. Don't mention it. Please." Nick sat back down at the table and signaled the waitress to bring him more coffee. "And ten or twelve aspirins? I think I feel a headache coming on."

The air was thick with smoke from the fires on the mountain last night. The smoke and fire from the old car was nothing compared to it. She knew the hospital would be clogged with asthmatics and other people with breathing problems. There were bound to be fire fighters who inhaled too much smoke or got burned by the sparks too. Not a good day to have to go to the emergency room.

Sharyn ran up the street to the courthouse. It would've been nice if all other county business would grind to a halt because of the fires and now, the new arson investigation. But everything else went on as well.

The commission was holding hearings that week on the fate of the old Clement's Building. They wanted her to testify about the security of the building. Fire raced through the home of the Capitol Insurance Company ten years ago and killed seven people. Capitol Insurance wanted the building to stay the way it was until the arson investigation was solved. But work on that case stopped years ago.

Her father, T. Raymond Howard, investigated it for over

a year. Every lead was another dead end. They knew the fire was purposely started but no suspects were ever charged. The case was closed, as far as Diamond Springs was concerned. But the insurance company hired outside arson investigators to come in. Eventually, they stopped that too.

The burned out building still stood on the corner of Fifth and Palmer. Teenagers and homeless people used its ruins as a hangout since she was in high school. Graffiti made it an eyesore. The county commission was eager to pull it down and have someone build something new.

With the huge influx of people into Diamond Springs, space was at a premium. The city needed all the tax dollars it could get. Capitol wasn't paying as much on the ruined building as another new owner would on a new building.

The commission was still getting ready when she walked through the door. The room was packed with people. The debate began as a heated argument between big business and a small town trying to move forward. It quickly escalated to a question of creating a memorial park for those people who died in the fire. The city thought they should sell the property to the highest bidder. The group of noisy protesters thought it should be donated for park space.

"Sheriff Howard," the new DA, Eldeon Percy, greeted her. Always immaculately dressed in a white linen suit, he was the epitome of the old-time southern gentleman. He was appointed to the position when the elected DA, Jack Winter, decided to run for the senate seat. Because of the county bylaws, he was allowed to keep the position for another two years before there would be an election.

"Mr. Percy." For Sharyn, the man represented the good old boy network in the city. She fought it since the day she took office. Questionable deals and backroom politics were its hallmark. She suspected but couldn't prove links to gambling, extortion and murder. Her private file was already a thick slab of documents that kept growing.

Jack Winter made it clear to her that he didn't want her there as sheriff. Instead, he offered her a position working with him in the DA's office. He also hinted that her father was involved in some of the suspect activities in Diamond Springs. Sharyn pushed ahead anyway, making some progress, hoping she wouldn't find anything that linked her father to them.

"I suppose you're here to testify?" Percy drawled.

"That's right, sir. Excuse me." Talking to him made her skin crawl. But at least he seemed to be happily married and didn't hit on her like Winter. Talking to him was frightening.

Ty Swindoll and Reed Harker were both county commissioners from the new developments outside the city. They liked to give Sharyn a hard time on a regular basis. Their budget cuts and warnings were always ringing in her ears. They cornered her before she could reach her seat. Both commissioners wanted to know what she was going to say when she testified.

"I'm going to tell the truth," she answered.

"The truth doesn't matter a whole hill of beans, Sheriff," Harker replied, glancing furtively from side to side.

"Your testimony could break this," the other commissioner told her bluntly. "We've got the Capitol people worn down anyway."

"A win here would look good for all of us," Harker assured her.

Sharyn faced the men squarely. "If you're ready for me to say that the building is a public nuisance and we'd be better off with something new there, no problem. That's my position."

Both men sighed. Harker shook her hand. "Not like we were asking you to lie, Sheriff."

Swindoll grinned. "We've got it, Sheriff. For once, we see things the same way."

She took her seat. Now that *was* a scary thought.

The protesters were a loud, noisy bunch that included many faces she knew from around Diamond Springs. Including her Aunt Selma. They already spent days holding hands around the building and lighting candles for the souls of those who died there. They'd tried everything to force the commission to give up the land for a park and a memorial.

Commissioner Betty Fontana brought the meeting to order. She warned the protesters that they would be thrown out if they couldn't be quiet. She was a slight, birdlike woman, possibly the only commissioner with any common sense. Ty Swindoll was a thorn in Sharyn's side since he took office from George Albert. He fought her at every opportunity. He denied funds to the sheriff's department and ragged on her about stupid infractions. Still he told her that she was doing a good job and promised to vote for her. Betty Fontana might also be the only sane commissioner.

When it was her turn to testify, Sharyn couldn't help noticing that the representative from Capitol insurance was looking a little frayed. Mark Goodson was only in town for the meetings. He was a young lawyer with a cheap suit and bad shoes staying at the Motel 8 up on the Interstate. Probably one of hundreds who worked for the company. He shuffled and re-shuffled his papers. When he stood up to question her, he spilled coffee on his table and had to take a few minutes to wipe it up. It was obviously his first case.

Sharyn answered the commissioners' questions by explaining that the old building was a hazard. Young people congregated there to do drugs and have parties even though the structure wasn't safe. Homeless people lived there and built fires in the basement when it was cold.

"Isn't it true that better police enforcement would stop these problems?" Mark Goodson asked her with a nervous smile.

"I assume you're asking my professional opinion?" Sharyn countered.

He nodded and looked around the room for any sign of support.

"Then no, it's not true. When I was a kid in high school, we used to sneak in through the loose boards. We were lucky we weren't killed. Capitol could assign security guards around the clock but they haven't. I can't spare deputies to babysit a place all the time. We patrol the area but it doesn't matter. In my opinion, the building should be leveled and something new should be there."

"But of course that's just your opinion," the lawyer added quickly.

"That's what you asked for, sir."

The young attorney sat down. His thin face was so dejected, Sharyn felt sorry for him.

"You're excused, Sheriff, thank you," Betty Fontana said with a gracious smile. "If there are no other witnesses, I think we should put it to a vote."

Sharyn left before the vote was taken. She could read about it later in the paper. She had more immediate problems than the Clement's building. While she was waiting to testify, the fire on Diamond Mountain was burning out of control. Their county emergency helicopter was joined by several others from surrounding counties dumping chemical foam on the fire. Two firemen were dead. Several others were injured.

Ernie met her at the front door. "Heard the reports?"

"Yeah, I had my earplug in during the meeting."

"Sam Two Rivers and Bruce Bellows are waiting for you in your office. Ed and Joe are out on patrol and answering a domestic disturbance call. There was a wreck on 7th street. A deer and a car. Cari's handling that."

"Good." She took a cup of coffee from him. "Thanks, Ernie. We need about ten more hands right now."

"The volunteers went home. I'm trying not to call them back in unless we have to. At this rate, the whole town will be exhausted before the fire's put out."

She nodded and took her coffee into her office. "Bruce, Sam. What can I do for you?"

Bruce Bellows was passionate about his job as wildlife manager for the area. Sam was his assistant, a Native American tracker, who helped the sheriff's office in a murder case in the mountains a few years back.

"Sheriff, we have to do something about the wildlife fleeing the mountain. Several populations could be wiped out before it's over. It's not so much the fire as when they get down here. We picked up two bear cubs this morning. Both dead. Shot by nervous home owners."

"Do you have a plan?"

Bruce glanced at Sam who nodded. "In some places, they use safety nets to catch the animals as they run from an area. We could string up nets on the mountain, especially in the areas where the larger wildlife are most affected."

"Do you have the manpower for it?" She didn't want to sound cold hearted but she couldn't commit people she didn't have.

"We have plenty of volunteers," Bruce assured her. "We can't get the permits from the county to do it. The commissioners want to do an environmental impact study. They say the nets could be a hazard to crews fighting the fires."

"Could they?"

"No," Sam denied emphatically. "The nets are taken down ahead of the fire line. It wouldn't do any good to have them burn, would it?"

It made sense to her. "What can I do to help?"

"Because the sheriff's department is also animal control for this area, you can say the nets are part of animal control. It would stop so many larger animals from running into town. And that would give us the chance to use them without the six week study."

"Okay. Consider it done. If anyone says anything else, send them to me."

Bruce stood up and shook her hand with gusto. "Thank you, Sheriff. This will help you out too."

Sam shook her hand too. He didn't let go when he was finished. Instead he looked at her hand then up into her eyes. "Do you believe in fate, Sheriff Howard?"

"Sometimes," she answered with a smile. "When it works in my favor."

He shrugged. "This is a fateful meeting. You won't regret this decision. And you will be re-elected. But you must pass through several trials first."

"Thanks, Sam. I think." She was glad when he released her hand.

He nodded to her. His dark face was shuttered but his eyes were piercing.

"Sheriff?" Ernie called her name a few minutes later.

"Yeah." Sharyn blinked and realized that Sam was gone.

"Are you zoning?"

"I guess." She rubbed her eyes. "Ernie, come up with some kind of permission form for Sam and Bruce to set up nets on the mountain to catch wild animals that are running from the fire."

"Okay." He put them out in front of her on the desk.

"Ernie—"

"What? They told me why they were here. I thought I'd be prepared."

"And you thought I'd go along with them?" She signed the forms.

"You're not a moron, Sheriff."

"Thanks. Sam said this was a fateful meeting and that I'd be re-elected to office."

"Great. He didn't read my palm!"

Sharyn laughed. "You didn't agree to do what he wanted. Speaking of which, Reed Harker and Ty Swindoll were pretty cozy this morning too."

"Yeah, I heard about that. The commission voted to sell the land and have something else built there. Apparently, they already have a buyer in mind. The building is scheduled for demolition in the next week."

"That's fast work."

"Gotta get it in before the election," Ernie reminded her. "Your polls are up two points today. People like your attitude. You stay calm in the face of difficulties like the fire and the accident."

"Still behind Roy, though, right?"

"Yeah. But you'll catch up. Maybe you could walk around town looking calm and that would bring you up a few more points."

"Polls don't matter, Ernie. All that matters are the votes."

"You're right, ma'am."

"Any luck on that serial number?"

"Yep. I traced it back to the owner. Brian Hammer. He lived over in the apartments off of Center Street."

"That's where the car was parked." She looked up at him. "You said *lived*?"

"He was killed in an accident in June. Which, I suppose, is why he didn't move his car in a while. No family we could find. The car was abandoned."

Sharyn scrolled on her desk calendar. "Any relationship to the man in the backseat of the car, you think?"

Ernie shrugged and scratched his head. "None that I can see. Unless the man in the backseat knew the owner was dead and crashed in the back because it was safe."

"That sounds unlikely. But I guess we'll know more when we know who the man was in the backseat. Any word from Nick?"

"Not yet."

"I'm going home for a few hours to sleep." She yawned. "I suggest you do the same. Things aren't going to get better any time soon. We're going to have to do this in shifts. Joe, Ed and Trudy can carry things here and tell Cari what to do."

Ernie yawned in response to her yawn. "Sounds good to me. I'll plan on being back in four hours to relieve the others."

"Me too. Maybe by that time things will calm down."

Sharyn talked to her office manager on the way out. Trudy nodded, too busy with calls coming in to answer. She managed to yell, "Have a good rest!" as Sharyn walked out the back door to her Jeep.

The house was quiet when she got home. There was a note from her mother. She was out making lunches for the volunteers fighting the fire on the mountain. Sharyn stripped off her uniform, gun, and boots and fell into bed. Within two minutes, she was asleep.

Three hours later, her phone was ringing. She answered and listened with half an ear. Someone was dead on the mountain. She signed forms for the nets to be put up. The press was going crazy. Roy was at the sheriff's office, demanding an explanation.

She hung up the phone, not really comprehending what they said. The gist of it was that she had to go back to work. All her tired mind could think was that they could have waited another hour and she'd be up anyway.

Despite the chaos Trudy claimed was going on, Sharyn took a few minutes to take a shower and find a new uniform. She brushed her hair until it gleamed, small curls dancing around her face. She clipped on her badge and put on her gun. When she looked into the mirror, she saw her father's face looking back at her, square jawed and steady eyed. For once, she didn't wish she were like her sister or her mother, tiny porcelain-like ballerinas. She needed her father's strength to handle this difficult time. She only wished he was there with her to handle it.

Her front yard was littered with candidate's signs. Several of them were hers since her mother decided that she wanted her to run for office. Several of them were for Jack Winter since he was a close friend of her mother's. His signs replaced Caison Talbot's re-election posters since her mother ended her relationship with the senator.

Sharyn shivered as she had a strange mental image of her mother dating Jack Winter while he was smiling suggestively at *her*. It was the product of too little sleep and being startled awake. Her mother counted Winter as a friend but she would never think about marrying him.

Slipping in through the back lot, she parked her Jeep and went inside the sheriff's office. Reporters littered the area around the office but they were barred from being inside. Every eye turned when she entered the main room.

"Well, Sheriff," Roy Tarnower greeted her with his big, booming voice. "While you were napping, a man lost his life on the mountain in the net you signed for to save animals. What do you have to say?"

She yawned, glad there were no cameras in her face. "I need a cup of coffee."

Chapter Three

The man was lying in the blackened orange clay. His fingers were locked in the mesh net. He wasn't badly burned like the man in the car. More scorched all over. His face was still recognizable. Mark Goodson. The lawyer sent to represent Capitol Insurance.

Ernie and Joe pushed back the crowd of spectators. Reporters already had their pictures and their stories. It was clear to everyone that the man became trapped in the net as he was trying to escape the fire that was racing up behind him. His shoes were burned. The path continued up his legs and back to his hair that was singed and smoking. His face wasn't burned but it was blackened by smoke. His eyes were open, looking out over the rolling mountains below him.

"Sheriff, were you advised that the nets might cause someone to be trapped up here?" one reporter fired at her. "Isn't it true that you gave permission for the nets to be put in place against orders from the commission to keep them down?"

Sharyn didn't answer. She didn't feel like bantering clever answers with the reporters today. She bypassed the crowd and went right for the body. Nick was already there working. He was dictating his observations to Megan who scribbled them in a notebook as they walked around the scene.

Megan looked up when she saw her. "Two guys toasted in two days. A new record for Diamond Springs."

Sharyn ignored her too. She crouched down next to the body and looked out over the smoke filled vista. "I guess this is pretty open and shut."

Nick knelt down next to her. "Megan, go to the car and get a tape measure."

"I want to help move the body!"

"Megan!"

The girl popped her gum and stalked off towards the car. "He's not a deer."

Sharyn glanced at Nick. "What do you mean?"

"Think about it. No matter how it looks, this net didn't kill this man. He had plenty of room to run around it. A deer panics and can't make those decisions. Look at the way the ground is scorched all around him. I waited to move him until you got here. If the ground isn't scorched *under* him, you'll know he dived into the net before the fire reached this level."

"So, something else killed him?"

"Help me move him."

Together, they carefully rolled the man away from the net.

"His hands are still pliable. He hasn't been dead for very long," Sharyn observed.

"And the ground isn't scorched under him." Nick showed her. "He might have been running, fell into the net, and had a heart attack. But he wasn't burned because the net was here."

She smiled at him. "Thanks."

"Anytime." Nick glanced up to see how close Megan was to them. "But you owe me dinner *out* somewhere. Just the two of us."

"Right. As soon as I have a free hour again." She studied Mark Goodson's body. "You know, it's only been a few hours since he lost his company's battle to keep the Clement's building upright."

"Lost? He let them have it," Megan replied. "He was the worst lawyer in the world."

Sharyn took out her notebook. "What do you mean?"

"I wanted the county to go for the park idea. We need some green space in Diamond Springs. He could've pushed for that. He caved. He let them take the property for half the fair market value. Didn't put up a fight for usage. Nothing. He was useless."

"I don't think that affected him dying," Nick advised. "Could we please stick to the subject?"

"Sorry." She shrugged and handed him the tape measure.

"The ground isn't scorched under the body. You can see from the front of his clothes that he fell before the fire got here. His hands and face aren't burned, just sooty from the smoke. I'll bet he doesn't have any smoke in his lungs," Nick said for Megan to record.

"But why was he up here?" Sharyn puzzled. "He's still wearing the same suit he was wearing this morning in court. He wasn't here to fight the fire. He sure wasn't here hiking and enjoying the scenery while the mountain was burning around him."

Nick had Megan took note of Sharyn's remarks. "We'll have to get him cleaned up to see everything. There's some blood on the side of his shirt collar. Let's roll him over again."

Sharyn watched while Nick examined the body more closely.

"Anything?" Ernie asked joining them.

"Nick thinks he was dead before the fire got here," Sharyn told him.

"What was he doing up here anyway?" Ernie asked. "Look at those shoes! You'd think even a big city fella would know not to dress like that up here. Those shiny flat soles wouldn't get him through this rough terrain."

"Well, it looks like he was struck from behind by a sharp, blunt object." Nick removed his gloves and gave them to Megan. "The skin is torn but it's ragged. I think it was more the force of the blow that cut him. The wound looks deep enough that it could've killed him. I'll know more after we get him to the morgue."

Ernie shoved his hat back on his head. "You mean he was murdered?"

"Unless a deer came up and hit him in the back of the head while it was trying to get away from the fire." Nick checked the ground around the body. "Lots of footprints. Too many. The scene was contaminated before I got here. We were lucky they didn't move the body."

Sharyn nodded. "Let me know what you find out."

"I'm still working on that burned guy in the car."

"Put this ahead of it," Sharyn said. "Let's find out what happened up here."

"You got it, Sheriff."

"Thanks, Nick. You too, Megan."

Ernie walked beside her as she left them with the body. "Are you gonna make an announcement yet?"

"They all know it's Mark Goodson?"

"Yeah. I called back to have someone notify his next of kin before it hits the AP wire."

She sighed. "Who found him, Ernie?"

He consulted his notebook. "Sam Two Rivers and Bruce Bellows. They came to check the net, found him and called it in."

"You talked to them already?"

"They had a load of animals on the back of their truck. I told them I'd catch up with them later."

"Okay. Yeah. I'll talk to the press." Sharyn climbed up on a blackened rock that put her above the crowd. "If I could have your attention, please?"

"Sheriff, are you going to say something useful or just the usual I don't know stuff?" Foster Odom asked in a brittle voice.

"I'm going to tell you what you already know, Mr. Odom. Mark Goodson was found dead here about an hour ago. He's being taken in for an autopsy by the medical examiner. We should know something more later."

"Does it look to be foul play, Sheriff?" another reporter asked her.

"I don't know yet. I'll have to wait for the medical examiner's report to comment."

"Did you authorize putting up the nets on the mountain, Sheriff?"

"Yes, I did. Bruce Bellows is our county wildlife manager. He recommended it. I'm sure all of you know that the meaning of the word wildlife has gotten out of hand in Diamond Springs since the fires up here. He thought the nets would save some of the animals and make it less scary for people in town."

"Did you know the county commissioners asked Mr. Bellows *not* to put up the nets?"

Sharyn considered the question. "Mr. Bellows came to me with the idea and asked me if I could give him permission to put up the nets. I told him I could and that the idea seemed to be a good one. We didn't have time for an environmental impact study. I'm told the nets have already saved some animals. None of us wants to find a bear eating our trash or hit a deer with our cars."

"Sheriff?"

"That's it," Ernie decided. "We'll know more later, like the sheriff said."

Sharyn walked through the barrage of reporters and questions.

Ernie jumped into the Jeep with her. "You okay?"

"I don't know." She started the engine. "I think its lack of sleep, stress, and too much smoke inhalation. I need a vacation."

He grinned. "Yeah. Me too. Maybe after the election."

"Maybe the election will give me one."

"We're not gonna talk like that. What do you think that boy was doing up here?"

"I don't know." Sharyn saw the medic team coming for the body as she drove down the mountain. The twisted roads were slick with rain and chemical foam. "Did he drive up here?"

Ernie looked at his notes. "I'll have Joe check before he comes down. If he did, it's probably a rental car so it should be easy to spot."

"Not so easy in that crowd."

"True. But when they clear out to follow you to the office and put their stories into their computers, it should be."

She smiled. "Ernie, I wouldn't miss this part if I lose the election."

"Maybe not *this* exactly," he argued comfortably. "But you'd miss the job. You know you would. You're good at it. Natural born, as your daddy would say."

"A week before the election, I have two dead men. One burned up in a car. The other only half burned up clutching a net that I authorized. Despite the commission's feeling that it shouldn't be up." Sharyn laughed as she turned out of the mountain access road. "You think that will get me elected?"

"I think the fact that you can think straight is one of your best assets, Sheriff," he assured her. "I'd vote for you. Even if I didn't work for you. You can't help that there's more crime. There's more people coming in from all over. The county wanted to grow. Diamond Springs wanted to grow. This is what you get when you grow a lot."

"I suppose that's true," she half agreed. "Guess Roy couldn't make it up the mountain fast enough, huh?"

Roy Tarnower passed them, driving like a demon towards the access road. When he saw her distinctive red Jeep with the sheriff's emblem, he stopped quickly and turned around to follow them.

Ernie whistled. "If there was time, I'd give him a ticket. How fast do you think he was going back there?"

"I guess he already thinks of himself as being the sheriff."

"Why?" he quipped. "Was the hot donut sign out at the Krispy Kreme?"

"He wasn't as bad as all that, was he?"

"I was a junior deputy while he was in office. He treated me like his go-fer. Ernie, get my shoes. Ernie, wax my car.

Ernie, date my daughter. Your daddy never treated another human being like his personal slave. I admired that about him. And I respect that about you."

"Thanks. I'm feeling better now. You can stop pointing out my good qualities."

"All right. Then my work here is done." His mustache twitched. "You know, Annie and I are thinking about getting married."

"Really? When?"

"When the election is over. Maybe a Christmas wedding. Nothing too big or fancy. She's already done it before and I don't think I can handle it."

"That's wonderful!" She hugged him when she stopped at a red light. "I'm so excited for you!"

He glanced out the window. "I know this is gonna sound stupid. You might not want to do it. But your best friend is supposed to be your best man. Since your daddy died, you and I have become pretty tight. I know you should be a bridesmaid or whatever you call them. But I'd like for you to be my best man. Or best woman, as the case may be."

"I'd be glad to do it. It will make my mom cringe."

"Oh, so you mean you're motivated?"

"She's been different since she and Caison broke up. Plus now, Kristie is going through 'everything is my mom's fault'. I think Aunt Selma is encouraging her. I feel sorry for her."

"The last few years have been pretty tough on her," he concluded. "She's a strong willed woman. Had to be to keep up with your daddy. With his murder and that awful thing with Kristie, not to mention her baby girl becoming sheriff and investigating her own daddy's death. It's been tough. She'll come out of it."

"At least she and Caison aren't together anymore."

Ernie looked at her as she pulled the Jeep into the parking lot behind the sheriff's office. "Are you sure that isn't the little girl talking who didn't want somebody to replace her daddy?"

Sharyn turned off the engine. "Ernie, it was Caison Talbot! Anybody but him."

"How about Jack Winter?"

She made a face. "Anybody but Caison Talbot or Jack Winter."

"Are you sure about that, Sheriff?"

"Don't start with me, Ernie!"

Deputy Cari Long met them at the back door. "Sheriff, I need to talk to you."

Sharyn hung up her hat. "Okay. We need to have a meeting anyway and—"

"Privately, please." The younger woman curled her arms protectively around herself as she walked back into the main part of the office. Her long, honey-colored hair swept across her face. She went quickly into Sharyn's office and closed the door.

Ernie waggled his eyebrows. "What's up there?"

"I don't know." Sharyn looked at her watch. "It's a little early but call David and JP in. We need to have a meeting about everything that's going on. Then we'll get going on checking out what happened to Mark Goodson."

Cari was waiting impatiently in the office. She was the newest deputy and the youngest. She started in the department working on the computers in the basement. Sharyn gave her a chance to work as a deputy when she found an important glitch that helped solve a case.

"What's wrong, Cari?" Sharyn closed the door behind her and sat down.

"I know this is going to sound stupid."

The phrase seemed to be contagious. "Try me."

"Sheriff, I know it was wrong to date David when I first got to be a deputy. I don't want to go into that." Cari was agitated, plaiting her shoulder length honey blond hair with her fingers and pacing the floor. "I broke up with him. Then I did something even more stupid. I started dating Ed."

Sharyn tended to agree with her that both decisions were bad but she wasn't there to pass judgment. "Go on."

"Now I don't want to date Ed anymore. He's too old for

me. He tries hard and he's cute but I need someone my own age. I want to go rollerblading and see stupid movies. I-I know this is a bad time right now with the election and the fires and the murder—"

Watching Cari twist her hair was painful. Whatever she was going to ask couldn't be as bad as that.

"Could you tell him? Let him down easy? If it came from you—"

"No!" Sharyn realized that she was wrong. It could be worse.

"He might hate me if I tell him. I swear I'll never date another man in this department if you'll do this for me. I don't know how to tell him. I think it could shatter him, you know? I don't want to ruin his life. I don't want him to hate me."

Sharyn got to her feet. "You're right, Cari. This isn't a good time. There's a lot going on."

"So you think I should wait and have you tell him after things get better? Because I could date him until then. It's not like I hate him or anything."

"No, Cari. I'm not going to tell Ed for you at all. You'll have to do this. And this is all the time I have to talk about it. I need you to get on the computer until everyone gets here. It's not official yet but we could be investigating another homicide."

"You mean the man in the net?"

"Yes. The man in the net. Mark Goodson. Contact Capitol Insurance and find out what they can tell us about him. We need to know about his life and his family. Anything that could help us. We need to know who to release the body to when the ME is finished."

Cari's eyes were stricken. "What about Ed?"

Sharyn hugged her briefly. "You'll find the words. Ed is stronger than you think."

They walked out of Sharyn's office together. Ed was standing at Trudy's desk, talking.

Cari turned to look at Sharyn. "Okay. I just hope he isn't maimed by it."

Sharyn hid her laughter in a tiny smile. "He'll be fine. Then get started on the computer, please?"

"She's coming this way," Trudy told Ed. "She's got that look in her eyes."

"Trudy, how long have you known me?"

She pretended to think. "Why, Ed, I think we've known each other for about twenty years. You started here right after my last baby was born."

Deputy Ed Robinson turned the full force of his remarkable blue eyes on her. His boyish face and curly blond hair belied his years. "Have you ever known me to be wrong about a woman?"

Trudy rolled her eyes. "Are you saying you didn't think she was 'the one'? You always think that about every woman you ever date! You said it about her over the summer. Every woman is 'special' and the 'right woman for you'. Until you break up. Which I think the longest record on that is about two months."

"I didn't know people were keeping track."

"We're not, you idiot! It happens all the time! Besides you wouldn't know a long-term relationship if it came up and bit you on the nose! You had two strikes against you on this one from the beginning."

"What? She was perfect for me."

"First." She counted on her fingers. "You work together. Always a mistake. Second, she's too young for you."

"Too young? I need a woman with some spunk, some fire. Besides, I'm young at heart." Ed smiled his devastating smile at her.

Trudy picked up some papers. She was immune to that smile. "Go away if you don't want to hear the truth. Older women can have spunk and fire too. You're afraid if you date someone your own age that you'll feel old. Dating someone young enough to be your daughter isn't gonna make *you* young, Deputy. But dating someone your age might make you happy for once."

Cari finally reached them. She held her head high and smiled at Ed. "Can we talk?"

By the time all the deputies of the Diamond Springs' sheriff's office gathered at the worn wooden table in the interrogation/conference room, it was almost six P.M.

An early dusk was falling over the city thanks to the heavy smoke coming down from the mountain. The afternoon edition of the Gazette featured an article from Roy Tarnower about what was wrong with the city right next to the notice about Mark Goodson's death on Diamond Mountain.

"We're going to have to start working in four hour shifts to keep up with everything," Sharyn told her deputies. "At least until we get some rain or they can contain the fires. With the wild animals, and the bad tempers and the possibility of evacuating the town, we need to be alert."

"What about the dead men?" David asked baldly. "Are we investigating two murders?"

"We don't have anything that points to the first burn victim being more than a bad accident," Sharyn explained to him. "Mark Goodson does look to be another homicide. We'll work that in shifts too as we can do it."

"How do we start?" JP wondered how it could all get done.

"We'll start with you and David. You'll work four hours then Ernie and I will relieve you for four hours. Joe and Ed will relieve us. Then we'll start over. Try to get some sleep in between shifts. You're going to need it. If the fire moves towards town again, we could all be called in to fight it. Cari and Trudy will be manning the phones on split shifts and Cari will also be working on the computer."

"What about the volunteers?" David whined about the weird hours. "Why can't they take up some of the slack?"

"We aren't going to call them in unless we need them for the fire. I don't want to exhaust all of our resources. This has the potential to get much worse."

"No," David protested. "Just *our* resources!"

Sharyn was glad to hear him going back to his usual cranky self. It meant that he didn't think he was in love with her anymore. That had to be a good thing.

"What about animal patrol?" Joe Landers leaned back in his chair. He ran his hand across his spiky dark hair "Am I responsible for animal control on all shifts?"

Animal control was a sore point for them all. Sharyn knew this but there wasn't much she could do about it until the commission reversed its stance and re-hired the animal control unit. "I talked to Bruce Bellows a few minutes ago. He said he and Sam with their group of volunteers will take over animal control until we get through this emergency."

"Good thing. I never want to see another scared raccoon again. I'd rather fight paramilitary groups then listen to that chittering!"

"Well for now, you're safe. You'll come in with Ed on the shift after Ernie and me." She turned her attention to the group. "Coordinate your shifts. Know when you're supposed to be here. No one has time to call or come and get you."

There was a short rap at the door then Nick joined them. His face was dark with weariness and a day's growth of black stubble. His white shirt was open at the throat. His tie was missing.

"You look like I feel," Ernie teased him.

"That bad, huh?" Nick joked back.

"None of us are a fashion plate right now." Ed looked specifically at Cari who blushed and looked away.

"I hope I'm not interrupting a pep rally." Nick put down a folder on the table. "Because we've got another murder to solve."

There was a general groan around the table.

"What's the matter? You guys want to see me out of a job?" Nick passed out copies of the report to them. "This is a preliminary finding on Mark Goodson."

"Somebody hit him hard enough to kill him?" Joe read from the paper.

"I think the murder weapon might be a shovel," Nick hypothesized. "We looked around for any sign of a weapon at the site. There was nothing there."

"If it's a shovel, you could look around up there for a year," Ed said. "There's only about a thousand or so."

"This would have to be a big one, pretty heavy." Nick sat down. "Not one of those kinds you put together in parts. We're talking a serious, heavy instrument. He must have been lying on the ground, face down. Someone came along behind him and used the shovel straight down. He probably crawled to the net and died. Not a bit of smoke in his lungs. The fire came after he was dead."

"The perp might've planned on us finding a burned body that would be harder for you to figure out," Joe entertained.

"Like the one in the car?" Ernie questioned.

Nick shrugged. "I checked out the back of the skull on the first body from the car. The same thought crossed my mind. But there was nothing there. The guy in the car burned himself to death, straight and simple."

"So we don't think the two incidents are related?" Cari dared in a low whisper. It was always difficult for her to jump into group discussions.

"Not at this time, Deputy. But I can't rule out anything until I have all the tests back on the first body. Right now, this is what we got. Mark Goodson was killed by a strong, sharp blow to the back of the neck. I'm ruling it a homicide since I don't see anyway it could've happened by accident."

Sharyn nodded. "Thanks, Nick. Okay. That's where we are. Everyone except David and JP, go home and get some sleep. Be back here for your four hour shift."

Cari hung back while the other deputies filed out. "He was devastated."

Sharyn glanced at Nick's curious face. "He was?"

The young woman nodded. "I knew he would be. I just pray that he recovers."

"Go home and get some sleep, Cari. I'm sure he'll be fine."

Cari smiled at Nick then left them alone together.

"What was that all about?"

"Cari wanted me to tell Ed that they couldn't date anymore because he'd be devastated by it." Sharyn smiled at him. "She was very concerned for him."

Nick laughed. "I suppose that's cruel. Maybe he really is devastated by it."

"I'm so sure."

"Speaking of being devastated." Nick purposely leaned against the light switch in the windowless room. "Oops."

"Nick, I—"

He gathered her close to him and kissed her solidly. Pent up emotion made them cling together. Their time together was fleeting and fragile.

"This is stupid," she whispered breathlessly as he kissed her neck and sifted his fingers through her hair.

"It is. And it's your fault," he whispered back to her in the darkness. "If you treat our relationship like a petty high school thing, it will be a petty high school thing. I'll be groping you in the morgue when no one's looking."

The light came on suddenly. Sharyn shoved him away from her. Nick dropped his papers on the floor and bent down to pick them up.

"Something wrong with the light in here, Sheriff?" Ernie asked, looking from one to the other.

Sharyn's face was hot. "I think I pushed against it then I couldn't find it again. Nick was helping me look for it."

"And I dropped my papers," Nick finished.

Ernie didn't say anything. But his mustache twitched and his eyes twinkled with humor. "Whatever you say, Sheriff."

"Thanks for doing that Goodson autopsy for us, Nick." Sharyn awkwardly reached out to shake his hand.

"No problem, Sheriff." He shook her hand, his clasp warm and sure.

"What's up with you two?" Ernie asked. "You got something planned?"

"Something like what?" Sharyn asked nervously. "We're just trying to be civil to each other."

"That's what I meant." Ernie studied both of them. "You look a lot like Cari and Ed when I caught them making out last week in the storage closet."

He left them alone again with a caution to watch out for the light switch.

"You never call me sheriff," Sharyn whispered as she corrected Nick.

"You never shake my hand."

She was breathing hard. "Don't ever do that again!"

"Fine. Let's have a real date. Nothing would make me happier. Besides punching David."

"Not *now!*"

"When? If now isn't good, when is good? As exciting as it may be kissing you in the interrogation room, I don't think I can handle that kind of exertion."

She played with putting a pen in her pocket. "What are you saying?"

"That we can't go on hiding and sneaking around. I want to take you out for dinner and a show. I want to see our names in the Gazette's gossip column. I'm too old for sneaking around pretending that I've never kissed you. Or that I don't want to hold you."

She could see the sincerity in the depths of his almost black eyes. She knew she pushed him for the past few months since they discovered that they wanted to try to have a relationship. But now really wasn't a good time. There was so much going on. And there was only another week until the election. "If we can make it through the next week, we'll start going out in public together."

"After the election. Right?" He demanded tersely, not sure if he liked the terms. Despite his warning, he knew he wasn't going to walk away. He'd waited too long for her.

"Right."

"Okay."

She touched his hand. "Thanks."

He smiled and gently touched the side of her mouth. "My pleasure."

"The county commissioners want to have a word with

you," Ernie told her when she went back to her office. "They called an emergency meeting and invited you to be the guest of honor."

"Lucky me." She picked up her backpack and started to put her things into it.

Ernie watched her. "Not planning to attend?"

"Not tonight."

"They might not take kindly to that attitude."

"I'm an elected official. I work with them, not for them."

He nodded. "That's a change for you."

"I'm tired, Ernie. I'm going home to take a hot bath and read a page in a book I've been trying to finish for the past year. One page at a time." She pulled her pack closed and settled it on her shoulder. "They can roast me tomorrow as well as today."

"I'll send your regrets. I'm going to talk to Bruce and Sam in the morning. Or whenever the next shift is that isn't midnight."

"Good idea. Good night, Ernie."

"Night, Sheriff."

Trudy and Ed watched her walk out of the office after telling them goodnight.

"I'm worried about her," Trudy confessed with a frown.

"She'll be fine," Ed retorted. "I'm the one with the broken heart. Why aren't you worried about me?"

"Because I *know* you'll survive. You always do."

Ed leaned his elbows on her desk. "You know, Trudy. I never realized how pretty your eyes are."

She laughed. "Forget it, Ed. I'm too old for that. And I've known you too long."

Ed smiled at her and tucked a strand of her hair behind her ear. "No one's *ever* too old, honey."

Chapter Four

Faye Howard was cleaning up from making dinner when her daughter walked in the side door. She stopped and stared in amazement. "You're home early."

"We're moving to four hour shifts," Sharyn told her, putting down her backpack. "I'm home until ten then I'm going back in."

"Would you like something to eat? I just put some vegetable soup away that Selma sent over. There's some cornbread too."

"Sure." Sharyn collapsed on the closest kitchen chair. "Thanks. Did you see Kristie today?"

"Yes. She's doing very well. I think she might be ready to go back to college for the winter term."

"Really? What does Aunt Selma think?"

Faye dipped some soup and rice into a bowl and put a piece of cornbread on top before she set it in the microwave. "Why doesn't it matter what *I* think? Why is Selma so much smarter than me?"

Sharyn searched for words. She didn't want to fight with her mother. She didn't have the energy. "I thought that Selma had a better handle on what's going on with Kristie. That's all."

"You mean because it was my fault that your sister became addicted to painkillers and started stealing things? I don't think that's fair."

"I didn't say that."

"You mean because I was too busy having a life of my own to notice that your sister was in trouble after that horrible man did those things to her? Or because I have a hard time looking at those scars on her without feeling like I should've done something to save her?" Faye sat down beside her daughter and burst into tears.

Sharyn had seen her mother cry before but never like this. Her mother was always careful that her face didn't get blotchy and that her makeup didn't smear. Now, big racking sobs shook her tiny frame. Even her carefully created hairstyle seemed affected by it. Tiny blond strands stuck out everywhere. She patted her mother's back awkwardly, not sure what to do or say.

"Your father used to do the same thing," Faye told her, sniffling. "You're so much like him. I wonder if there's any of me in you? I look for it. Just something small, you know? I'm glad I'm not a man and that I gave birth to you or I wouldn't be sure you were my daughter at all."

You mean not like Kristie? Sharyn bit her lip to keep from saying it out loud. "No one blames you for what happened to Kristie. Bad things happen sometimes. Even if you weren't planning your wedding to Caison, it would've happened anyway."

"Kristie has problems. I've accepted that." Faye nodded. "Problems Selma can help her with but I can't. You know, you were always close to Selma as a child. Kristie wasn't like that with her. I think because she's more like me. You and Selma should've been mother and daughter, I guess."

Sharyn didn't know how to answer that. She got up and took her plate of food out of the microwave.

"Want some tea?" her mother asked her.

"Sure. That would be great."

Faye poured her a glass of cold tea and plunked down a few ice cubes in it. "Why can't we talk? Why is there always this distance between us? I feel like I don't even know you. Except that you're so like your father I can guess what you're going to do next."

Sharyn swallowed a mouthful of beans and rice then took a sip of tea. "I don't know. I don't feel like there's a distance. I mean, we live together."

"Now. But if I'd married Caison, we wouldn't. Or would you have considered living with us?"

"No!" Sharyn cleared her throat. She didn't mean to be so sharp with her. "I mean, no. I wouldn't want to leave the house empty. Plus my work is here."

"Caison won't win this election against Jack," Faye predicted with a tight smile on her face. "He's not even trying. He's a beaten man."

Sharyn smiled at her mother. She couldn't help it. She looked like a raccoon with her eye makeup smeared. "I-I'm surprised you aren't helping him."

"He lied to me. I could put up with everything else. But he lied to me. In all our years of marriage, your father never lied to me." Faye pulled herself together and patted her hair into place. "I'm going with Jack to a rally tonight. I know you don't like him. I don't think we should discuss it."

Sharyn ate her cornbread in silence. She agreed with her mother. She didn't want to talk about her going out with Jack Winter. She didn't even want to think about it. "Thanks for dinner."

"You're welcome, honey." Faye kissed her forehead. "We're going to have to try harder in the future, aren't we? I loved your father even though I never understood him. I love you too."

Even though I don't understand you. The words were implied in the trail of perfume she left behind as Faye left the room. Sharyn finished eating, rinsed her plate and glass then fell into bed in shorts and a sheriff's department T-shirt. The single page of the romance novel she was reading would have to wait. She set the alarm for an extra fifteen minutes for a quick shower when she got up. She was asleep before she pulled up the sheet.

Faye came in a short while later to tell her goodnight and found her that way. "She works so hard."

"She does," Jack Winter agreed with her, looking at the sleeping woman on the bed.

Faye sighed and pulled up the sheet then readjusted her green silk dress. She smiled at Jack then walked out of Sharyn's bedroom.

Jack lingered a minute longer. His gaze caressed Sharyn's body outlined by the sheet. He touched a strand of her bright hair and inhaled the fragrance it left on his fingers. "Sweet dreams, Sharyn."

The sheriff's office was quiet when Sharyn went back at ten o'clock. Ernie was there on the computer. Cari was waving a sleepy goodbye. JP checked with her to make sure when he was supposed to come back in.

"I'll call you," David told him.

"That's the blind leading the blind," Ernie remarked without looking up from the monitor.

David frowned at him. "I'll be here at ten tomorrow."

"You'll be here at six or I'll be out at your place with a ball bat!"

David counted up the hours. "Yeah. That's right. Okay."

Ernie shook his head and laughed.

"What's so funny?" Sharyn asked, joining him at the computer.

"You missed it. I was just fooling with David's mind. That's all," Ernie replied.

"Don't confuse him again! He's just getting out of being in love with me."

"And you're glad, huh?"

"More than I can say," Sharyn answered.

"You're that sure about Nick?" He hit print on the key-board.

She shuddered. "It doesn't matter. I'd rather be alone than with David."

"We won't get into that," Ernie promised. "I have some info on Mark Goodson. Cari has turned into a right smart information gathering machine."

"Great. You know I have the money to hire one more deputy trainee."

"I know." He faced her. "Anyone in mind?"

"Well, actually—"

"What are the two of you doing here?" Marvella announced herself. She took off her jacket and hung it up in the janitor's closet.

"Marvella?" Ernie couldn't believe his ears.

"That's right, sweetie. I'm here!"

"I wasn't talking to you!"

"You said my name," she corrected him. "You were either talking to me or about me. I can tolerate the first but not the last."

Sharyn smiled and lowered her voice. "She's finishing college in a few weeks. She's a hard worker. She knows more about what goes on around here than I do. I think she'd be an excellent candidate."

"She has no background in law enforcement. She's a pain in the neck. She drives everybody crazy. I think I'll have to take early retirement if she's here all the time."

"You've been threatening that a lot lately. Something up with that?"

He shook his head. "No, not really. I think I'm afraid it might happen. What would I do with myself?"

"You've got that shipbuilding hobby."

"Exactly." He watched as Marvella began twirling around the office with her duster. "Marvella, huh?"

"JP had no background in law enforcement either."

"You're right. Let me know what happens. Maybe I can beef up that shipbuilding hobby."

"You'd drive Annie crazy. I'll let you know what happens. She might not be interested."

"And for the record," Ernie said, "I know more about what goes on around here than anyone. Including Marvella."

Sharyn laughed. "Okay. I won't argue that point. What about that info on Goodson? Anything useful?"

"Maybe." He shrugged. "His mother was his only relative. They informed her of his death five minutes before she saw it on CNN. It was an interesting death with the net and all so it was picked up by the networks."

"At least she knew ahead of time, even if it was only a few minutes."

"He was thirty-four, got a law degree from UNC-Chapel Hill. He lived alone. No pets. No girlfriend as far as anyone knows. He was divorced, no children. They tried to reach his ex-wife but she's out of the country on a honeymoon cruise."

"That takes her off the suspect list," she remarked with a yawn.

"Yeah. JP went and had his motel room sealed off. His rental car was still parked in the lot there. He paid his bill and was ready to leave. The desk clerk thought he left until they went to clean his room and found all his stuff there. Lucky for us they waited and didn't pack it up for him."

"So, whoever killed him transported him up the mountain?"

"Probably. It's a workable theory anyway."

"The only other possibility is that he went up there on his own and someone killed him. Maybe he met someone up there."

"Or it was an accident and someone got scared."

She shook her head. "The way Nick sounded, it didn't seem like an accident. I think we should go over to the motel and take a look around."

"We might as well," he agreed. "It's pretty slow here. Chief says the fire is contained for now. A thousand acres have burned already up there. Can you believe it? Weather forecast is calling for some rain. Maybe we'll get lucky."

The Super 8 motel on the interstate cutoff to Diamond Springs was nothing to brag about. Clean, cheap lodging, nothing fancy.

The night clerk was also the owner. He let them into the room. "No one touched a thing, Sheriff. You don't think he was murdered here, do you? I wouldn't want to get a reputation like the Bridge Motel, you know?"

"I don't think he was murdered here, Mr. Caywell," Sharyn assured him. "We'll need forensics to go over the place in the morning but it doesn't look like anything happened here."

"Thanks, Sheriff. I invested my family's savings into this. I don't want to lose it all."

"I understand. Thanks for your help."

When he left them alone, Sharyn and Ernie pulled on gloves and started to look through the room.

"One suitcase," Ernie said, putting it down on the bed. "The man traveled light."

"He was very clean," she observed in the bathroom. "All the towels are folded. No hair in the sink. No toothpaste on the mirror."

"Think they cleaned up anyway?"

"I don't think so. There's garbage in the trash cans. He used the coffeemaker and the soap is open and used on the sink. But no coffee rings on the tables. And the bed is folded up nice and neat. Selma would say he was brought up right."

"Look at this." Ernie held up his hand and a shower of tickets spread out on the bed.

"What are they?"

"Gambling stubs from Harrah's casino."

"That's interesting."

"Looks like he played while he was here too."

She looked at the racing forms that were in the suitcase. "I think we found Mark Goodson's hobby."

"Pretty expensive too," he added thoughtfully, seeing the amounts that were placed as bets.

"He was a lawyer," she replied. "He could afford it."

"Let's find out."

They left word at the front desk that nothing in the room could be touched yet. The rental car couldn't be moved either until they could establish that Goodson wasn't killed in the car. Caywell was nervous but accommodating. His only request was that they didn't mention where the dead man was staying.

"It's too late for that," Sharyn told him. "Maybe it won't matter to anyone who doesn't live in Diamond Springs."

"Thanks anyway, Sheriff."

"If you think of anything helpful." Ernie left his card. "Let us know."

"I talked to my staff. No one saw him with anyone out of the ordinary."

"We might want to talk to them too," Sharyn said. "We need a list of names and information on your employees."

"I could fax it to your office."

"Thanks," Sharyn replied as they left the motel.

"He was helpful," Ernie acknowledged.

"You mean as opposed to Marti Martin at the Bridge Motel?" Sharyn laughed as they climbed back into her Jeep with the single suitcase in tow for the evidence locker.

They drove past the hospital on the quiet streets of Diamond Springs. It was almost too quiet. There wasn't a sign of life anywhere.

"Looks like Nick's still burning the midnight oil." Ernie noticed the light on in the basement morgue.

"Let's stop by," she suggested. "Maybe he has something for us."

They parked the Jeep in the empty hospital parking lot. Smoke from the fire hung in the air like fog. It rasped in everyone's throats, and left clothes and hair smelling acrid.

"This smoke is kind of eerie, isn't it?" Ernie whispered in the cool night air.

"Yeah, like a bad horror movie."

"And here we are going into the morgue. Oooooo!"

Sharyn shivered but she laughed at him. "Do you turn into a werewolf or do I?"

Nick was putting Mark Goodson's body back into the cooler when they arrived. "Good timing." He snapped off his gloves and removed his white lab coat. "You're gonna love this!"

"I hate when he says that," Ernie groaned.

"It always means trouble," Sharyn replied.

Nick grinned at them. "That's me. Trouble is my middle name. Come into my parlor."

Sharyn felt that grin and the sound of his voice zoom down through her and tickle her toes. "I can't believe you're still here at this time of night."

"I told you I have midterms that have to go out, and be graded and recorded before the Christmas holidays. Half of my students have some bug that's going around. I've been called up on the mountain twice in the past twenty-four hours for fire brigade duty. I have to get done with this."

He sat down behind his big desk. It was so cluttered with papers that the desktop was invisible. Sharyn sat in a chair by the desk. Ernie looked questionably at another chair before he sat on the sofa.

"I appreciate the effort," she replied politely.

"Put it in the paycheck," he growled. "Or better yet, the county budget. I'm still waiting to get test results back on that first guy."

"If we're gonna start moaning," Ernie answered, "I've got some grievances."

"Okay. Fine." Nick took out his notes on Mark Goodson. "I already told you what killed him. He wasn't burned anywhere. He was pretty badly beaten though. Lots of bruises so it happened before he died. I'd say a few hours before. He had a black eye, a couple of cracked ribs, some damage to his nose and jaw. And I did some X-rays that were interesting. Both of his hands were broken."

Ernie shook his head. "I must be getting old."

"Why?" Nick glanced at him while he was putting the X-rays on the fluoroscope.

"Because two and two make four."

"Would you like to translate?" Nick appealed to Sharyn.

"We found gambling receipts from Harrah's and some racing forms from here in his suitcase. How recent were the breaks?"

Nick shrugged as he pointed them out on the X-rays. "Pretty recent. Maybe early this year. They were healed but it hasn't been long. No arthritis either. This man was going to have some serious arthritis when he got older."

"Well we spared him that agony, didn't we?"

Sharyn and Nick both looked at Ernie.

"What? Arthritis isn't any fun."

"So you think the broken hands were from bad gambling debts?" Nick asked Sharyn.

"It wouldn't be surprising. Anything else we should know?"

"He had a fractured tibia at some point but that was a long time ago, maybe twenty years. He had an overbite. He was borderline diabetic. He was starting to lose his hair. And he took wild yam before he was killed."

"Wild yam?" she asked, scribbling in her notebook.

"Probably for constipation. Some people get it when they travel."

"Is that it?" Ernie scratched his head and yawned.

"Except that he's dead, yep. That's it."

Sharyn closed her notebook. "He led a pretty uneventful life. Except for the gambling."

"Maybe that's why he gambled," Nick observed. "To jazz up his life."

"Maybe." She studied his dark face. "You look tired. You should go home and get some sleep."

"What are you guys doing out this time of night? Where's David and JP?"

"Four-hour shifts." Ernie yawned again. "The sheriff volunteered us to take this one."

Nick and Sharyn both yawned with him.

"That's enough of that," Sharyn protested.

Nick's phone rang. "Joe's Pool Hall. Eight Ball speaking."

Ernie laughed and shook his head.

Nick listened for a moment then replaced the receiver. "No rest for the wicked. That was my volunteer fire unit. We're going up on the mountain again."

"Is the fire worse?"

"No. They had the idea that if they keep people out there

24/7 maybe it won't get bad again. Glad I got that done on Goodson. I'll let you know when something turns up on the first guy."

"We better get back too." Ernie nudged Sharyn. "It's been too quiet. I'm beginning to wonder when the zombies come out."

"We're not that far from Halloween," Nick told them. "Anything is possible."

"You're right. Good luck, Nick."

"Thanks, Ernie."

Sharyn walked outside with Ernie. When they reached the Jeep, she stopped suddenly. "I think I dropped my notebook in there. I'll be right back."

He nodded and climbed into the Jeep. "I'm not sure right now which one of us the zombies would get first. Helpless sleeping man in Jeep or pretty young thing going back into hospital. You better hurry."

She ran back into the morgue as Nick was turning out the lights in his office.

"Sharyn? Is something wr—mmpphh."

She kissed him hard and fast on the mouth, wrapping her arms around him and hugging him tightly. "Be careful up there, huh?"

"Yeah."

"Call me."

"Yeah. Sharyn?"

She turned back to face him when she reached the door.

"I told you it would come to this. Making out in the morgue."

"Not now, Nick."

She was gone, disappearing into the night. He pulled on his old New York Knicks jacket and shook his head. "Not now, Nick. Not now."

They got back to the office in time for Ernie to understand why there were no calls. Marvella was on the phone with a man who couldn't find his cow. "Sir, it's almost midnight. What do you expect anyone to do about your cow before morning?"

Ernie snatched the phone from her. "You're not with the sheriff's office yet!"

Marvella stared at him like he'd gone insane. "What do you mean *yet*?"

"Never mind," Ernie growled, turning his attention to the man on the phone.

Sharyn sat down at Cari's computer desk. "I've been meaning to talk to you about that Marvella."

"I'm ready to graduate, sugar. I know you love me around here but I'm not taking any permanent janitor position."

"I was thinking of something more like a deputy sheriff trainee."

"Trainee?" Marvella balked. "Why not a full fledged deputy? I could run rings around Ed and Joe. I won't even start on David!"

"I have to start you as a trainee," Sharyn told her. "But I'd like to have you here."

Marvella smiled, showing even white teeth. "You're serious, right?"

"Yep."

"Gun, badge, car? The whole enchilada?"

"After training."

"How long is training?"

"Six weeks in the office, six in the field. You have to pass a couple of tests. We check your background."

Marvella shook her head. "I don't know, Sheriff."

"Think about it," Sharyn persuaded. "I believe you'd be good at it."

"You mean you'd trust me at your back with a gun in my hand?"

"Anytime."

Marvella held out her hand. "You got yourself a deal. Can't start until January though."

"I'll have Trudy get the papers ready."

Marvella whooped as she left the office.

Ernie muttered, "It's a sad day in Mudville. I can't believe you did that."

"Why?"

"I don't know. I just can't believe it. Maybe it's sleep deprivation."

"Maybe. What about the cow?"

"I told him we'd give Sam and Bruce a call in the morning. He was happy with that."

"Good. Let's see what we can find out about Mark Goodson's credit history, huh?"

Mark Goodson was mortgaged to the hilt on everything. His credit cards were gone. He was in a credit-rebuilding program but dropped out. His divorce papers cited that his wife left him because he used their house and everything else as collateral on a gambling loan. She told the court that he was 'obsessed with gambling. Addicted to it.' Medical records showed that he was in the hospital earlier that year for two broken hands.

"Claimed he got them skiing." Ernie read as Sharyn took notes.

She sat back in her chair. "So he was a bad gambler who kept going and getting in deeper and deeper."

"Pretty much." Ernie ran his hand across his eyes. "He was probably in contact with Chavis Whitley. That's probably where he got those racing forms."

"Good old Chavis." Sharyn arrested him regularly for breaking the gambling codes. From horse racing to cock fighting, he was on top of it all in Diamond Springs.

"Tell you what." Ernie glanced at his watch. "We got another hour and I'm gonna go to fall asleep sitting here. Let's go and see if we can roust him out so he can tell us that he never met Goodson."

"Sounds good to me."

Chavis Whitley was from a well-known local family. They disowned him years before when he couldn't stay away from gambling. He lived with different women in a small house at the edge of town. His father left him the property so that it couldn't be mortgaged to finance his gambling.

"Old man Whitley knew what he was doing, I guess." Ernie stretched and put his nightstick in the holster on his side before he got out of the Jeep. "He could've left some money for paint."

Sharyn did the same with her nightstick. Chavis was never an easy man to question. Invariably, he ended up going to jail for assault on whatever deputy brought him in. He was a big man with quick fists.

His current girlfriend, a pretty slip of a girl named Patti, was eager to tell them where he was. "They locked him up."

She answered their question then went back into the house, leaving the door open. Sharyn glanced at Ernie who shrugged. They followed her carefully into the house.

"Where?" Ernie asked, not surprised to find him in jail. Just surprised that it was someone else's jail.

"Up at Harrah's. I'm heading there now with bail money."

"What did he do?" Sharyn questioned her.

Patti shrugged her thin shoulders. "They said he was cheating at some game. That's so stupid. Chavis never cheats. He's the best. He doesn't have to."

"Do you recall Chavis mentioning a man named Goodson?"

She stopped stuffing clothes into a backpack. "You mean the dead guy?"

"Yeah. That's him." Ernie pulled on his gloves and wandered around the room. "Ever hear his name?"

"Only on TV."

"When did Chavis go up to Harrah's?" Sharyn tried to discover if he had an alibi during the last twenty-four hours.

"He went up this evening about six. And that's another stupid thing. Even if he was cheating, they couldn't catch him that fast. He barely got up there when he called to tell me he was arrested for cheating." Patti flicked her tawny colored hair out of her face.

So there was no alibi. Chavis was probably in Diamond Springs when Goodson was killed. Murder was something that wasn't on his rap sheet yet. But the way the man lived, it was always possible.

"Mind if we take a look around?" Ernie asked her with a sweet, fatherly smile.

"Don't you need a warrant or something?" Patti demanded tearfully. "I mean, I don't know about any of this. I want to do what's right. But I don't know anymore."

He put his hand on the girl's shoulder. "You talk like you're from Charleston."

She sniffed. "That's right. Mount Pleasant, actually. But I met Chavis in Charleston. Worst day of my life. Sometimes, you make bad choices, you know?"

"You need bus fare to get you home? I bet your mama and daddy are worried about you."

Patti broke down sobbing. Ernie let her cry on his shoulder. Sharyn didn't touch anything but she looked around the house. On the kitchen table, there were huge stacks of tickets from Harrah's like the ones they found in Goodson's motel room. Some of the tickets were dated for the same days. Chavis was in Cherokee at the same time as Mark Goodson.

Ernie helped Patti finish packing. She gave them permission to look around Chavis' house as much as they wanted. "I've got this money for his bail."

"You leave it there," Ernie advised her. He gave the girl a hundred dollars. "He'll come after you if you take it. That's the honest truth. You need to leave here clean. You don't need that kind of money. I'm sure he'll call someone else who can come get him."

"Thanks." She hugged him impulsively. "I'm going now before I change my mind. Or Chavis changes it for me."

"Good luck." He watched her get in her old Mustang and drive away. "What's the attraction for girls like that? Why would she want to be with that loser?"

"I don't know. Some women like tough guys." Sharyn

waited until the girl was gone to show Ernie the betting receipts. "They might have been together up there."

"Or they could've been there at the same time and never saw each other," he answered. "That's a big place up there. You ever been?"

"Nope but I'm thinking we might need to go up there and take a look around."

"I was thinking the same thing. I'm not telling Annie that's where we're headed though." Ernie laughed at the thought. "She thinks it's gambling when they forecast the weather on TV."

"Wonder what she'd think about Patti crying on your shoulder just then?"

"She wouldn't think anything. She knows she's the only woman for me."

"Don't worry," Sharyn teased him. "I won't tell her and ruin all the marriage plans."

Ernie eyed her suspiciously. "Speaking of which, just what was going on in the conference room last night?"

"You mean yesterday?" Sharyn nodded to the clock on the wall that was striking midnight.

"Don't change the subject."

"What was going on?" She hedged, stooping down to check out a stash of cash hidden behind the sink in the kitchen. "I told you what happened. What else could happen?"

"You and Nick were making out in the conference room."

"What?"

"I saw a strand of red hair caught on his jacket when he was leaving." Ernie watched her face closely.

Sharyn turned away to examine a dirty curtain. "Really?"

"Sheriff, you don't have to sneak around. Everyone knows you're dating."

"The election committee doesn't think so."

"What do they have to do with it?"

Sharyn stripped off her gloves. "They think it's a bad time for me to have a public romance."

"That's crazy."

"That's what happens when you want to get re-elected. They think they own your life."

Ernie shook his head. "You're right. Things will clear up after the election. I told Ed no making out in the office. Same goes for you."

She decided to ignore that remark. "I think that's about all we can do here without a search warrant."

"She let us in the house and told us to look around." Ernie was glad to comply with the change of subject.

"But she isn't even his wife. I don't think it would hold up in court. We can get a search warrant and have Ed and Joe check it out while we're gone."

"That works for me," Ernie agreed tiredly. "Our shift is over anyway."

"So I'll pick you up at ten tomorrow at your place. We'll have to split the shifts while we're gone. It's only a few hours up anyway."

"Great," Ernie replied happily as they left.

The next morning Ernie's girlfriend Annie called Sharyn at nine thirty and told her that Ernie was sick. "He's burning up with fever and other things I don't want to talk about, Sheriff. I don't think he can come in today."

Sharyn held the phone to her ear while she buttoned her shirt. "Okay, thanks Annie. There's some kind of bug going around. Tell him I hope he gets better fast. We're too busy for him to be sick right now."

Annie laughed. "I will, Sheriff. Thanks."

Sharyn hung up the phone and decided to check in at the office before she left to make sure everyone knew what was going on.

Sam Two Rivers was waiting for her when she got there. "Heard you were going up to Harrah's. My brother is the sheriff up there. Mind if I tag along?"

Chapter Five

Sharyn was glad for the company on the trip to Cherokee. But when Sam was silent for the first hour of the trip, she decided to speak up. "So your brother is the sheriff in Cherokee?"

"That's right."

"It must be a lot different now than before the casino was built." She tried to pry a response from him.

"It is."

The casino was on Native American land deeded to the Cherokee Nation. The multi-million dollar business was owned by the Cherokee but run by a syndicate. The Cherokee Nation got a share of the proceeds from the gambling. But many claimed it came at a high cost to the spirit of the people.

"Sam, is it me or do you have a problem with the world in general?"

He glanced at her. "The world in general. I don't have a problem with you, Sheriff Howard."

"I'm glad to hear it. How did you get away from Bruce?"

"He has plenty of volunteers. I have an emergency at home."

She thought talking to Sam would be easier. "I'm sorry. Anything I can help with?"

He shrugged. "My brother was shot by a man trying to escape from jail."

"Is he all right?"

"He's recovering. It was in the shoulder. Years ago, we would've gone after the man and taken care of the problem. Especially a white man. Today, we let the police take care of it."

"Is his name Chavis Whitley?"

Sam was surprised. "Nobody mentioned you were psychic, Sheriff. How'd you know?"

"I was going to see him about the murdered man in the net." She filled him in. "Do you know if he was caught?"

"Oh, he didn't get away. My brother shot him in the knee. He dragged himself out to the street and got in a car but they got him."

"You know, I called the sheriff's office before I left this morning. They didn't mention a word about this."

"We're pretty tight-mouthed when it comes to handling our own affairs. They probably thought you were a Fed or something."

"How long has your brother been sheriff in Cherokee?"

"About five years. I told him it was stupid but he has this civic pride thing going on. My whole family is like that. That's one of the reasons I don't live there anymore."

"Instead you live on Diamond Mountain and help animals." Sharyn was surprised to get so much out of him.

"Yeah. They think I'm stupid. But I did my civic duty in the army. I don't owe this country anything else. Animals need help. They can speak for themselves but we've forgotten how to listen. I try to be that bridge between our two worlds."

"You believe that animals talk to you?"

"Crazy, huh?" He laughed, his copper-skinned face crinkling around the eyes and mouth. "Yeah, everyone thinks so. But they each have their own language. Like us, they are individuals and deserve autonomy."

"That's a powerful statement."

"I know. I keep it to myself mostly. You're a good listener, Sheriff."

"Call me Sharyn, please. We've known each other a while. We've worked together before."

"Yeah. That weird bear case on the mountain. I knew something was wrong with that one. Remember? I told you."

"I remember," she admitted. "Any thoughts on this one?"

"I can tell you it wasn't a bear or a deer that killed that man. And it wasn't the nets either."

"I didn't think so."

"The commission does. I read it in the paper this morning. You did the right thing, standing up to them. They're a stupid, wasteful group of people."

She laughed. "Who I'll have to answer to at some time. I might be elected by popular vote but they hold the purse strings for the county. I want to have something to give them besides the net theory. That works best with them."

"You're wise beyond your years. I think it might be your father's spirit that stands so close to you."

"Are you psychic now?" she asked lightly but a chill rushed down her spine at his words.

"No. Just more observant than most. Turn here. It's the fastest way into town."

The road was little more than a rutted track that disappeared into some trees on the side of a mountain.

"Maybe we should stick to the highway?"

"Wise but not adventurous. You have this Jeep. What do you think it was designed for? Its potential is unused cruising the streets of Diamond Springs."

"All right," Sharyn agreed shifting gears, "we'll be adventurous."

Sam sat back in his seat and surveyed the land. His large beaked nose dominated his profile as she stopped to glance at him when they reached a fork in the road. "Where to?"

"To the right. The other way leads up to the reservation."

She had to use both hands to guide the vehicle safely out of the trees, across the foot-deep ruts and cracks in the clay road. They reached the center of town quickly but

Sharyn knew she wouldn't come that way again unless it was an emergency.

"My brother is at the hospital. The man you want might be there as well. Let me use your cell phone and I'll find out."

He identified himself to the person who answered at the sheriff's department. Sharyn listened as he nodded and asked questions. He finally closed the cell phone and turned to her. "They're both at the hospital. We should go there."

"Thanks."

"Glad I could help. I appreciate the ride up here. I don't own a car. Bruce lets me borrow his but he needs it right now. Don't use that phone anymore than you have to. It will kill you."

"What?"

"The cell phone. It's okay to use them once in a while but they aren't good to use all the time. People will be dying years from now, regretting their constant use."

"Thanks." It was all she could think to say to him. Sam was a strange man with some odd ideas but she liked him.

The hospital was tiny. Cherokee wasn't a big place. Until the casino was built, its only claim to fame was a small museum that highlighted the Cherokee history. There was a theme park nearby and some white water rafting. The land was extravagantly beautiful but the people were poor. The area was ripe for development.

It was raining when they reached the hospital. "I wish this would come down our way." She followed Sam across the street.

"It will when it's time," he answered. "Rain comes as it will. The animals know this. They plan for it the best they can."

Sharyn couldn't debate that. She went with Sam to visit his brother first to avoid any other mix up between the Diamond Springs sheriff's office and its Cherokee counterpart.

There were two big men at the door to Jefferson Two Rivers' hospital room. Both men stared at her and moved to block her from entering. Sam said something in Cherokee to them and they moved away. They entered the pale green room together and Sam introduced her to his brother.

"Welcome to Cherokee, Sheriff Howard," Sheriff Two Rivers said, cradling his injured arm. "I've heard about you from my brother."

Sharyn glanced at Sam who shrugged and looked away. "I hope it was good."

Jefferson nodded. "I'm happy to finally meet you. What can I do for you?"

She explained about Chavis Whitley. "I need to question him. I know you'll want to keep him here to stand trial for your assault. I don't need to take him back to Diamond Springs."

"Good. Please, feel free to question him. Do you think he killed this man?"

"I don't know. Obviously, he's graduated up a step in shooting you. It was only a matter of time."

"So you think nothing can change a man's path?" Jefferson asked.

"I think a man can change his path if he chooses, Sheriff. But my grandfather used to say that a caterpillar doesn't get butterfly wings because he thinks he should have them."

Jefferson laughed. "Very astute! Just ask one of the men outside the door to step inside. I'll have him take you to the room where they're holding Whitley."

"Thanks."

She walked down the corridor with the big man who was assigned to help her.

Chavis was surprised to see her. "You here to take me home, Sheriff?"

"I'm afraid not, Chavis. I'm here to ask you some questions."

"What's my reward for answering? I mean, where's my motivation?"

Sharyn sat down beside the bed and studied his unshaven, dirty face. "I can't do anything about the mess you're in here. But I can save you from another mess that might be waiting for you back at home."

He grinned, showing gold teeth in his mouth. "You mean Patti?"

"I mean Mark Goodson."

"Mark who?"

"The man you placed bets for while he was in Diamond Springs. The man you spent time with here at the casino."

"I don't know who you mean, Sheriff. I never heard of the man. I hope to be struck dead if I'm lying. I don't know him."

She shook her head.

"What? What's he done? Besides gambling."

"Gambling is still illegal in Montgomery County. Mark Goodson isn't facing gambling charges though."

"So? What is it?"

"He's dead, Chavis."

He looked around the room and moved his injured leg a little even though he grimaced at the effort. "I think it might be time for my pain medicine. I got shot in the knee, you know."

"Yeah, I know. So you don't know Mark Goodson? You never placed bets for him?"

"Never."

"If I find out different, I can't help you," she warned quietly. "If you want to tell me the truth now, maybe we can work something out. If you killed him but it was an accident, the court would understand that he owed you money."

"Yeah right." He frowned. "I don't know this dude anyway. I can't help you, Sheriff."

She got to her feet. "All right. Enjoy your stay."

"Sheriff?"

"Yes?"

"Have a nice trip back home. Send Patti up with that money."

"Patti went back home. You'll have to find someone else."

"That little—"

Sharyn walked out of the room. Despite Sam's warning about cell phone use, she went outside and called the office. "I need you to get a search warrant for Chavis' house. The car might be up here. I'll have to check that out with the sheriff."

"Everything's quiet here," Joe told her. "Except that the commission wants your head."

"They'll have to wait like everyone else," she told him, gazing out over the town of Cherokee. "I'll see you when I get back."

Sharyn got permission to take a photo of Mark Goodson around the casino. She wanted to know if anyone remembered seeing him there, alone or with Chavis. One of the bouncers remembered throwing Chavis out for cheating but didn't remember seeing Goodson. A pretty cocktail waitress remembered seeing Chavis and Goodson together. She told Sharyn that Chavis was consoling Goodson because he lost heavily at cards.

Another trip back to the casino put her in touch with the dealer who was at that game. He put Chavis and Goodson together in the casino on the night before Goodson came to talk to the commission. He said that Goodson lost a lot of money. He also thought that Chavis loaned him more to use in the game.

Sharyn left Cherokee with the man's name and phone number in her pocket. Sheriff Two Rivers didn't know anything about Chavis having a vehicle there. Sharyn called the state highway patrol and put out an APB on it. Sam was staying with his brother for a few days so she drove back alone. The drive was usually pretty long but she knew she would be facing the commission when she got back. That made the miles speed by. At least she had something to show for the effort.

Joe called her before she reached the office to let her know that they were going through Chavis' house. "Ernie dragged himself out of bed. He thought you might want to come on over here."

"Wouldn't miss it," she agreed, changing lanes to head for Chavis' house instead of the office.

"There's a commissioner at the office waiting for you anyway. I guess the idea is to escort you to the meeting since you ditched them."

"Thanks. I definitely want to help with the search. Which commissioner is it?"

"I don't know, Sheriff. They all look alike to me!"

She laughed. "I'm five minutes from the house. See you soon."

Joe was at the house with Cari and Ernie. Ed was on patrol and handling a possible robbery at a jewelry store in the new Lakeside Galleria.

"Nice to be doing some real sheriff's business." Joe was wearing his military type sunglasses even though there wasn't any sun. "I didn't sign up to chase cows."

Cari was tagging and bagging everything she could find that might pertain to the case. Already there were six bags of gambling receipts. "Hasn't this man been arrested before for gambling?"

"Plenty of times," Joe told her.

"You'd think he'd give it up and do something else."

"You'd think. But the criminal mind is different than yours and mine, Cari," Joe educated her. He was taking a course in understanding criminal intent and loved to lecture on it.

"I'm too sick to hear all that, son." Ernie sneezed and pulled out his handkerchief to wipe his nose.

"You sound like you should be home in bed," Sharyn remarked. "If your head was any more congested it might explode."

"I think it already did." His cell phone rang. He turned to Sharyn as he answered it. "This is it. We found Chavis' ride."

"Highway patrol?" she guessed as he finished the call.

"Nope. It was towed to our impound lot yesterday. Parked illegally at the mall. He didn't pick it up."

"Do we have a warrant?"

"Not yet."

"Let's go. We can pick one up on the way."

But Judge Dailey wasn't in a mood to grant any more search warrants that day. "I can understand the house, Sheriff. But the car? How could it be involved?"

"Because we believe that Chavis might have transported Goodson up the mountain. We need to have a lab run some tests on it to know for sure."

"Your honor, if I may intervene?" the assistant district attorney stepped up. "I believe the sheriff has good intentions and the vehicle is already in the sheriff's impound lot. The man has been arrested many times for various violations of the gambling code. Granting a search warrant for his house and car seems reasonable."

"To you perhaps, Mr. Fisher. To me it sounds like harassment. I won't issue another search warrant unless something from the house leads them to the car. Or they have some concrete evidence that the car was involved somehow."

"Yes sir." Toby Fisher shrugged his thin shoulders. "Sorry, Sheriff. You'll have to make do with what you have."

Sharyn had already counted to one hundred. Judge Dailey was always difficult. But he usually worked with the DA's office very closely. Not agreeing with assistant district attorney Fisher might signal an end to that. Dailey was in Jack Winter's pocket but the new DA might be a whole different ball of yarn.

"Thanks anyway." She shook his hand. "We'll work it out."

Ernie sniffled as they walked back out into the gray haze. "I think we should go and take a look at the vehicle anyway, Sheriff. There might be something we can tell about it from the outside."

"You're right. It's worth getting caught at the office."

"You mean the commissioner? If we sneak real quiet in the back, he might not know we're there."

"Good call." She smiled and patted his back. "Are you sure you feel up to this?"

"You wouldn't believe what Annie was doing to me at home. I'd rather tangle with a hungry bear running from a fire than have her try to make me well. Besides, it's just a little head cold."

"Okay. Let's go."

They walked in through the new back annex of the courthouse. It was almost finished and ready to use. Prisoners being taken to court wouldn't have to walk out on the street anymore. They could take them from the sheriff's office to the courthouse without running through a barrage of reporters or angry citizens. It would also keep the prisoners and the deputies out of the weather.

"You know I never figured Chavis for a killer," Ernie remarked as they skirted pieces of Sheetrock and electrical wire.

"I know. I was surprised at him shooting the sheriff in Cherokee. Maybe he's passed some invisible line. It happens."

"Even then," he argued, "he shot the sheriff in the shoulder. He could've aimed for the heart."

"Maybe he tried and missed."

"You got your daddy's sick sense of humor too." Ernie shook his head. "I ever tell you that before?"

"I think you've mentioned it a few times."

They made it through the annex and into the impound lot before someone noticed them. Charlie saluted from his shed by the back door. "Hi Sheriff. Deputy. Looking for something in particular?"

Ernie shushed him but it was too late.

Reed Harker stuck his head out of the door. "Sheriff? We've been waiting to talk to you!"

"You'll have to wait a little longer, sir." She walked right by him. "I'm on official sheriff's business."

Commissioner Harker followed right after them. "I was sent to bring you back."

"Oh brother," Ernie muttered. "Sounds like he gets a bounty or something."

"They might be doing that with the extra taxes now," Sharyn joked. "Which car belongs to Chavis?"

"A brand new red Dodge Durango." Ernie looked around the impound lot. "I knew I was in the wrong business."

Harker followed them out to the back of the lot, yapping at their heels. "Sheriff, the commission isn't going to put up with this. You should be concerned. Especially in an election year."

"I'm more concerned with solving this murder, sir. Charlie, do we have the keys for this?"

"No, ma'am. But I got a dealer key that will open it."

Ernie glanced at her. "No search warrant?"

"I know. I thought if we see something suspicious that might pertain to the murder, we could use our discretionary authority to look inside."

"That's skirting the line pretty closely."

"Are you doing something illegal?" Harker demanded. "I'm not going to stand here and allow the law to be abused."

"Best go inside then, sir," Ernie chided him. "Otherwise you might become tainted."

Harker held his ground. "I'm waiting for the sheriff."

Sharyn was walking around the Durango. It was dusty and full of ash like every other car in Diamond Springs. "No sign of any significant damage from the fire if he was up there."

"There's mud on the tires and sprayed on the back. Not many places to splash mud besides that area."

"That's not good enough, Ernie."

"Yes, ma'am."

"Are you looking for an excuse to break into this car?" Harker asked them in disbelief. "Is this the kind of thing that goes on around here?"

"Mr. Harker." Charlie handed a set of keys to Ernie. "You're gonna have an apoplexy out here like this. You might as well come back inside. Let the deputy and the sheriff do their job. They protect *you*, you know. Suppose this was your brother or son who was killed. Wouldn't you want them to do whatever they could to find the killer?"

Commissioner Harker thought about it. "The sheriff still went out of her way to ignore the commission's decision."

"Not ignore," Sharyn defended while she continued to look at the Durango. "I did what I thought was best for animal control. Remember? You gave me that authority when you made my office take over that job."

"There should've been some more consultation done," Harker fumed. "Time to assess the situation and look at all the possibilities."

She turned to him. "Sir, with all respect, there wasn't time for that. Animals and people were in danger. I made a choice to help them both and I stick by it."

"But that man was trapped in that net and killed, just like we feared. What if his family sues the town, Sheriff? Will you be paying for that out of your pocket since it was your decision?"

"He wasn't killed in the net, Mr. Harker. Someone took a shovel and deliberately killed him with it. They beat him before they did that. The capture nets didn't have anything to do with his death. He just happened to be next to one when it happened."

"We think it might be over bad gambling debts, sir," Ernie continued. "A local man is our suspect. He just shot the sheriff in Cherokee. He's being held there right now. This is his car."

"Oh." Harker looked at the Durango like it turned into a snake.

Sharyn stood back from the car. "We think Mr. Whitley took Mark Goodson up the mountain in this. We don't know if he was alive or dead at that time. Forensics will be able to tell us but Judge Dailey won't give us a search warrant. So we have to decide if there's enough evidence that we can see from the outside to warrant us going into the vehicle."

The commissioner peered into the car. "And is there?"

Ernie chuckled. "Well, sir. I can see from out here that there's a gas can in the back of this vehicle. The back seat is folded down like it was used to carry cargo."

"There's also a shovel," Sharyn reported. "It's stained with something dark. It's hard to tell what. There's ash and leaves all over in there. Some of them have some flecks of red on them."

"That sounds promising." Harker warmed to the idea. "Can you open it up like that?"

Sharyn looked at Ernie. "Considering that the shovel could be the murder weapon. And the red on those leaves could be blood."

Ernie wiped his nose. "But that doesn't link to the gambling lead. If the search is bad, even if *all* of Goodson's blood is in here, a good lawyer will get it thrown out."

"Is that true, Sheriff?" Harker asked her.

"I'm afraid so, sir. I'm going to call Joe and Cari. See if they've found anything."

She made the call while Ernie prowled around the outside of the Durango with Charlie and Harker beside him. "They didn't find anything that they could link back to the car."

Reed Harker grinned like a possum. "Maybe I can solve that problem. Look in here, Deputy."

Ernie looked in the back door on the driver's side. "You're a good investigator, Mr. Harker. More tickets from the casino, Sheriff. Lots of them."

"So that links the car with the house. That's the whole circle." She picked up her cell phone. "Mr. Percy, please."

"I thought you'd just break in and search it," Harker said disappointed.

"She's right." Ernie fingered his mustache. "The Judge said we could have the warrant if we could prove how they fit together. If we can make a case against Chavis, we don't want to lose it because we're impatient."

"I had no idea it was so complicated." Harker shook his head.

"It's for your own protection, sir," Ernie explained to him.

"But it helps people like Chavis."

"Sometimes."

Cari and Joe brought the warrant with them on the way back from the house. Before they got there, Harker and Charlie watched Sharyn and Ernie go through the vehicle. Sharyn called Nick to bring his team to go over the Durango. They bagged fifty betting stubs from Harrah's, some cash under the seat, and a few racing forms. They were careful to leave the back alone until Nick arrived.

"Oh good," he said a short time later. "An audience."

Megan and Keith led several other students to the car with bags, gloves and tweezers.

"Pay particular attention to the back," Nick told them. "I need a sample of everything. Carpet fibers, paint flecks. Any hair or tissue you find. Take some of everything and make sure it's all clearly labeled. Last week, I couldn't tell if I was looking at hair samples or sushi."

"They look like students," Harker confided to Sharyn.

"They *are* students," Nick whispered back.

"Should they be doing the work?"

"Does the commission want to put the money into hiring two full-time assistants?"

Harker backed down. He sat on the hood of another car and watched them proceed.

"What's he doing here?" Nick asked Sharyn quietly.

"He's taking me to the commission for a trial before they hang me."

"But those stupid nets didn't have anything to do with Goodson's death."

She shrugged. "I know that. I'm going to take this other information to them. But I don't think it will matter. They still think I overstepped my authority by letting Bruce and Sam put up the nets."

"The town is burning, people are dying and the county commissioners are preening in the mirror." Nick grimaced but he knew the realities of Sharyn's life.

"Well, at least there's only one homicide."

"I got the reports back from Raleigh this morning while you were gone. I tried to call you but your cell phone wasn't answering."

"I was at the hospital in Cherokee with Chavis and Sam Two Rivers' brother who is the sheriff there. What's up?"

"What did you find out?"

"You first." She smiled at him.

"Okay. I hope yours is good because you're not going to like mine. The dead man in the car was Montgomery Blackburn."

"Monte?" Ernie heard the name and joined them. "What about Monte?"

"He was the man in the car, Ernie. I'm sorry."

"He's the vet who lived under the Clement's building, right?" Sharyn recalled meeting the man earlier in the year.

"Twice decorated for bravery during 'Nam," Ernie told her. "Guess you were right about the idea of a homeless man getting into the car."

"He was doused heavily with whiskey. Probably inside and outside. There was some cigarette ash on his clothes. It was a bad combination."

"But not murder?" Sharyn questioned him.

"I don't think so," Nick agreed. "My theory? He was drinking heavily. Climbed into the back of that car with his bottle. It spilled all over him. He ignored it and lit a cigarette. The whiskey was the good stuff. He caught himself and the car on fire. Probably kicked it out of gear and it rolled down Main Street."

Ernie held his head down for a silent prayer then looked up again. "Poor old Monte. He was bound to go out in a bad way like Willy."

Sharyn put her hand on his shoulder. "I'm sorry, Ernie. I know he was your friend."

A wide-eyed young student came to Nick with a large bag full of leaves from the back of the Durango. "I think these have blood on them, Professor."

"Good. Put them with the others." Nick shuddered. "The boy gets into his work."

"I've got the shovel bagged," Megan reported, holding the item. "But I don't think this is the murder weapon."

"Why's that?" Sharyn asked the girl.

"Well, the angle of the shovel is wrong. There's some dark greasy substance on it that could be blood but I don't think it is. It isn't heavy enough either." She used the shovel for a demonstration. "Not enough downward thrust."

"Thanks," Nick said. "We'll check it out anyway."

"Those children are frightening, Dr. Thomopolis," Reed told him.

"I know." Nick grinned. "That's what I like about them."

Sharyn decided it was time to report to the commission. "I have to go. Let me know if you find anything, huh?"

"Always." Nick waved but didn't look at her.

"I'm going by Monte's place," Ernie told Sharyn. "It isn't much but I think his stuff should be buried with him."

"Wait for me," she persuaded. "I won't be long. I don't want you to go alone."

He agreed. "I'll walk up to the courthouse with you. I don't think I can come inside though. It might make my cold worse."

The commission was overwhelmed by the evidence against Chavis Whitley being responsible for Goodson's death. It didn't excuse Sharyn's actions with the net but it did satisfy their fears of being sued by the man's family. Reed Harker was an unlikely ally. He explained the process she went through, how her hands were tied and she did the best she could in the situation.

"We'll agree not to censure you, Sheriff," Ty Swindoll said after conferring with Betty Fontana and Charlie Sommers. "This time."

Sharyn didn't stick around to find out what that meant. Technically, they couldn't do anything but withhold her paycheck. She was elected by popular vote. They could give her a hard time and withhold funds but they couldn't take her out of office. If she was convicted of a crime, the

DA's office would handle the aftermath. Otherwise they were all smoke and no fire.

Ernie waited in the hall for her. "You don't look too chastened to me."

"Let's go before I forget how to count any higher."

"Try counting in another language. JP is teaching me to count in Spanish."

She laughed. "You're a good man, Ernie. And a good friend."

"Yes, ma'am. I was just looking at the Gazette society section. Seems like your worst nightmare is coming true, huh? I could swear I hear Caison Talbot bellowing all the way from his place!"

"My mother with Jack Winter?" Sharyn straightened her spine as they walked out of the courthouse. "I don't know. I think she's purposely trying to date men I don't like. I wish she would've decided to date you before you found Annie again."

"Whoa! That's not fair! I like your Mama and all but I don't want to marry her!"

"Why not? Then you could be my step daddy."

Ernie shivered all over. "A goose ran across my grave when you said that! Please, Sheriff. I'm an old man. I could have a heart attack."

"You know, Nick asked me once if you and I were—"
"*What?*"

She nodded as they rounded the corner of Fifth and Palmer. "I know. I told him I thought of you more like my father."

"That would be more than I could handle! Why'd he ask you that?"

"I don't know. It was a long time ago."

"Only one reason a man asks a woman a question like that." Ernie chuckled wisely. "It must've happened when he found out he was crazy about you."

"Really?" She pretended not to know. "When was that?"

Ernie swept his gaze around the basement they were entering. "Probably the day he met you. Monte kept his stuff around the front there. He wasn't worried about anybody stealing from him. He had a system."

"What kind of system?"

He crouched down next to what was left of the old boiler in the basement. "He kept everything in here. Claimed the kids were too scared to open it." He turned the handle and opened the heavy iron door. Inside were the bits and pieces of one man's life. A deck of old playing cards. Some letters on good stationary. A commendation from the Marines. His medals. A piece of blue glass. And a handful of gambling tickets.

Sharyn knelt down next to him. "Nick might have to rethink his theory."

Chapter Six

"Why?" Ernie turned his attention to the tickets she found.

"These tickets are from Harrah's. The same date that Chavis and Goodson were there."

"It doesn't surprise me any that Monte gambled but can you imagine him in that casino?"

"No." She studied the tickets, wishing they could tell her what she needed to know. "But what if he went along for the ride? What if he knew what happened between Chavis and Goodson? Maybe he became a liability."

Ernie took the rest of the trinkets from the boiler. "So Chavis rolled him into the car, poured whiskey on him and lit him on fire?"

"Yes."

He shook his head. "These tickets don't prove that. It could've happened like Nick said too. It could've been a drunken accident."

Sharyn snapped her fingers. "That's what's been missing! I knew something was bothering me."

"What is it?"

"Where was the bottle? If he spilled the whiskey on himself and lit himself on fire with a cigarette, where was the bottle?"

"I don't know. Are you sure it wasn't in the report from the fire department?"

"No." She took out her cell phone and hit speed dial. "But I can find out."

Chief Wallace told her that he wasn't sure where Melinda was. "She did the work and filed the report. You'll have to talk to her."

"How's the fire situation?"

"Slowing down finally, I think. Don't quote me on that. Every time I think things are going our way, the wind finds a new way to blow and it starts all over again."

"Thanks, Chief. Could you give me Melinda's number?"

Ernie was too sick to go on any longer that night.

"You've already worked more than we were supposed to." Sharyn insisted on dropping him off at his house. "Maybe things will get back to normal for a while. Take it easy and listen to Annie for a change, huh?"

He sneezed. "Yeah. Then I couldn't ever leave the chair by the fireplace! I'll talk to you tomorrow. Thanks for helping me get Monte's stuff. Let me know what you find out about the car?"

Sharyn finally got in touch with Melinda. She agreed to meet her at the garage where the burned car was being stored while the case was being resolved.

"What's your theory, Sheriff?" Melinda asked her as she pulled open the garage door.

"I was wondering about the bottle. If Nick's theory is right and Monte fell asleep after spilling whiskey on himself and lighting a cigarette, where's the bottle?"

Melinda switched on the overhead light. "I suppose it would still be in the car."

"Probably in the front seat or under the seat," Sharyn added. "Could we check?"

"Sure. Sorry. I didn't do a search of the car for the report. I thought it was pretty open and shut. Once I found that the accelerant was whiskey, I thought that was enough."

Sharyn pulled on some gloves. "It just came up. There was no way for you to know."

They donned masks and started searching through the

car. There was no sign of a bottle or any glass on the floor or seat.

"Could it have melted?" Sharyn asked her.

"Not hot enough. The body wouldn't have burned so completely except that the accelerant was mostly on it. And maybe inside of it, like Nick said. It also had a head start on the car's interior."

"I think Nick would've noticed if there was glass on the body. There wasn't a bottle in the car."

"What does that mean?" Melinda wondered as she stripped off her mask and gloves.

"It means that someone else did this. It means that this becomes a homicide instead of an accidental death."

"Any suspects?"

"I think the suspect for the killing in the mountains might be responsible. Monte might have seen something he wasn't supposed to see. Like Mark Goodson going to Harrah's with Chavis Whitley."

"The lawyer from Capitol Insurance?"

"Exactly."

Melinda shrugged. "Not a big loss. Lawyers are such maggots."

"I'm sure a lot of people would agree with you. Some people feel like he could've pushed harder for the land to be used as a park."

"Yeah."

"At least it won't be a fire trap anymore. Not that it mattered much to us when we were in school, huh? I used to sneak in there every weekend until my father caught me. I can't imagine why it was so cool to be there!"

"I wouldn't go in there." Melinda shuddered. "It was too gross thinking about all those people who died there."

Sharyn laughed. "I guess that was my problem, too. I didn't think much back then. Thanks for your help, Melinda."

"Anytime, Sheriff. I hope this case is easy for you to solve."

Sharyn missed a message from Nick. The metal walls of

the garage must have interrupted her signal. She called him back. His answering machine said he was grading exams in his office at the college and couldn't be interrupted. His voicemail clicked off as she got back in her Jeep and headed over there.

JP called her and asked what shift he was supposed to be working.

"You and David work until midnight. Then come in for your normal shift tomorrow night. The Chief says the fire hazard is down so let's lengthen those shifts and see if we can get back to normal."

"Okay, Sheriff."

"If Cari or Trudy are there, tell them to go home and come back tomorrow morning."

"Sure thing."

"Thanks, JP."

She called Ed and Joe and asked them to come in from midnight to six and to take the next day off unless she called them. They both agreed. It was almost 10 P.M. when she pulled into the college parking lot. With any luck, she could be home and in bed by midnight. Then she could be at the office with Trudy, Cari, and Ernie the next morning. Banning emergencies, they could be back on schedule.

She thought the school would be empty except for professors grading midterms. But there were plenty of teachers and students. There were still classes going on.

She knocked on Nick's door a few times. He didn't answer. She tried the handle and found it open. The large office was dark except for the pool of light on his desk. He was asleep on the papers he was supposed to be grading. His arms were folded under his head. His black-rimmed glasses were slipping down his nose.

Sometimes, she was still in awe that this man cared for her. They fought for so long. Maybe that was why it was so hard for them at first. For a long time, she didn't think she was going to be able to work with him at all. Now, she was worrying about him and kissing him goodbye, at least when nobody was looking. Things would be different after the election. It grated on her nerves that she let the election committee tell her how to live her life. But they were the experts and she wanted to win the election.

She leaned her face close to his and kissed his cheek. He groaned and blinked his eyes. His hand came up and knocked his glasses off. She caught them before they hit the floor.

"What time is it?"

"A little after ten."

"I have to get these papers graded."

"You were sleeping when I came in. How 'bout some coffee?"

He raised a dark brow. "Can we risk it?"

"We can have coffee without people talking."

"Are you sure? Because apparently breakfast was too intimate since you had to bring Charlie and Ernie with you."

"They were hungry."

"Me too." He drew her into his arms and kissed her. "You smell like smoke."

"Everything smells like smoke," she answered softly.

"This is more specific. You smell like burned car smoke."

"Wow. You're good. You could be making some money with that nose."

He kissed her again. "Do you know this is the longest you've stood still and let me hold you? Most of the time, it's like trying to hold on to a live wire."

She smiled. "I didn't realize I was so exciting."

His black eyes became serious. "You have no idea."

The door to his office burst open and the two of them sprang apart. They stood on opposite sides of his cluttered desk. No one would ever guess they were in each other's arms just seconds before.

"What is it?" Nick demanded impatiently.

"We're having a pizza party downstairs, professor. You should come. Bring your friend. Is that a real gun?"

"Yes, it's a real gun, you twit! She's the county sheriff. And I don't want any pizza. Go away."

"Sure. Sorry." The student backed out of the room and closed the door.

Nick put his hands to his face. "I'm getting as bad as you. There's a noise and I scramble for my safe corner."

"It won't be for much longer," she promised.

"Sharyn, do you really think people aren't going to vote for you if they know you're dating me? Where's the logic behind that?"

"There's no logic behind it. It's politics. You encouraged me to run for re-election. What's the point in me having an election committee if I don't listen to them?"

"I don't know. I'm sorry. It's probably not that. There's just so much going on and I think I've slept about four hours in the past week."

"The election's only a week away now. I'm sorry I put you through this."

"You're worth waiting for." He cleared his throat and began to shuffle the papers that were on his desk. "I assume you didn't come by specifically to have coffee with me so what can I do for you?"

"I thought about the fire department report on the car. I just got back from checking it out with Melinda. There was no bottle and no glass in the car. I think Chavis might be involved with Monte's death too. Ernie and I found gambling tickets in Monte's stuff under the Clement's building. They were dated for the same day that Chavis and Goodson were in Cherokee together."

Nick put on his glasses and took out his notebook. "I called you earlier. When you didn't answer, I thought maybe you went home for the night. We found carpet fibers on Goodson's body that matched the fibers from Chavis' Durango. There was no blood on the shovel. It was 10/40 motor oil. And I think Megan was right about the size and weight of the shovel. It isn't your murder weapon. But there was blood on the leaves and grass we took out of the back. It's consistent with Goodson's blood type. I won't have complete DNA on it for a few days but I think it's a pretty good bet that it matches. We also picked up two complete prints from the back that match his."

"That does it then. I can't make him on Monte's death yet but that's a pretty strong case against him for Goodson's death."

Nick shrugged. "I don't know how you're going to pin him to Monte's death. That's it, at least from my end."

"Thanks. Maybe we'll get lucky and he'll confess."

"Yeah."

Silence dropped like a wall between them. Nick fumbled with his papers. Sharyn put away her notebook.

"Well." She smiled and felt like an idiot. "I guess I'll go home now. Unless you want to reconsider coffee?"

"No, I don't think so. I really need to get these papers graded. Let me know what happens with the case."

She looked at his tired face. "I will. I'm trying to get the department back on schedule tomorrow. Don't push yourself too hard, Nick. I'll talk to you later."

"You take it easy too. Let's hope this fire thing eases up, huh?"

"Yeah."

Sharyn was halfway down the hall when she heard him call her name.

"I changed my mind." He pulled on his jacket. "If coffee's the best I can get right now, I'll take it."

Sharyn thought she'd be asleep as soon as she got home. Instead, the events of the past two days kept her up.

"I thought you said you were tired," her mother remarked as she tied her robe around her waist. "What are you doing up at this hour?"

"Couldn't sleep."

"Your father was like that sometimes. So exhausted he couldn't sleep."

"I remember." Sharyn looked around her father's office that they called a den when he was alive. Everything was the same as the day he was killed at the convenience store a few miles down the road. She liked to sit in there when she was confused or uncertain. It made her feel close to him.

Ever since she found Jack Winter there a few months before, she spent a lot of time sorting through her father's files. There was a thread of something that couldn't be traced running between her father, Caison Talbot, and Jack Winter. They worked together for years. In many ways, they ran Diamond Springs. Sharyn didn't want to think that her father was involved in any of their questionable activities. When she found Jack there, she wasn't so sure.

Knowing that he was spending time with her mother made her uneasy. It gave him access to the house again. She wanted to move faster looking through her father's papers but her job was too demanding. She figured whatever he was looking for wasn't easy to find. Was it evidence her father had against him? Was it something that would link her father to the ex-DA's crimes?

"Well, it's almost 5:30. I suppose you're going in at six o'clock?" "Yeah. Mom?"

Her mother sat down in a chair by the door. "What?"

"Was there anything going on between Jack, Dad, and Caison that might be illegal?"

"That's crazy! Your father wouldn't be involved with anything against the law. I don't believe Caison or Jack would either. Where do you get these ideas?"

Sharyn sighed, exhausted. She should've known better. Her brain must be out of order. "I don't know. Thanks anyway."

Her mother stood up again. "Would you like some breakfast?"

"No thanks, Mom. I'll just have some coffee at the office." She went through the normal activities: showered, brushed her teeth, got dressed. She was beginning to feel like a zombie in a bad horror movie.

Ernie called to tell her that he was much better and that Cherokee county was arraigning Chavis that morning.

"I'll call Sheriff Two Rivers. I think we're going to need to bring him down here for questioning."

"Sounds like a good idea. I'll see you at the office."

Sharyn made the call. Jefferson Two Rivers was back at work and ready to oblige her. He promised to send Chavis back to Diamond Springs as soon as the arraignment was over. She brushed her hair and picked up her gun. Her limbs felt like lead. She felt a cold coming on but went to work.

"You look kind'a sick, Sheriff," Charlie observed as she pulled into the parking lot.

"Yeah." She sneezed. "I feel kind'a sick too."

"Drink some bee balm with honey. Make you feel right as rain."

"Sheriff?" Ernie met her at the back door with coffee and a stack of papers to sign. "You don't look so good. Caught my cold?"

"I think so. What did you do to get over it so fast?"

"Annie made me eat rice and oranges. Don't ask me why. But I guess it worked."

"Sheriff, I need to talk to you about our arrangement." Marvella was there behind Ernie.

"I told you to wait," Ernie reminded her.

"I did wait. You were taking too long!"

"That's okay." Sharyn sniffed and sneezed.

"You sound awful! Take some warm honey and lemon in water," Marvella suggested. "Maybe *he* could get it for you while we talk."

"Ernie, would you get me a couple of Tylenol, please?"

"Sure thing."

Sharyn sat down behind her desk. "What's wrong, Marvella?"

"It's about the whole uniform thing. I've seen the way they look on you. Honey, I can't wear something that looks that bad! Can we compromise? Maybe I could wear brown and tan. Just not the uniform."

"I'm afraid not. It goes with the job. But if it makes you

feel any better, you get them for free and we send them out to be cleaned."

Marvella considered it. "I suppose that's not so bad. I was telling Ed and Joe about it last night. I don't think they believe it."

"They'll get used to the idea."

Marvella got to her feet. "I won't keep you, Sheriff. But I appreciate your confidence in me. When do I get my gun?"

Sharyn blew her nose in a tissue. "You'll have to complete your first six weeks of office training then take a gun safety class and get some shooting time out at the range. There's a test for that. Then you'll be issued a gun."

"All right. Take care of yourself." Marvella studied her with a shrewd eye. "I think something else is wrong with you, sweetie. That cold might have you down but I think there's something else. Man trouble? That hunky medical examiner giving you fits?"

"Please," Sharyn whispered, "I'm trying to keep it out of the papers. Everyone here knows. Just not the public at large. Not until after the election."

Marvella waved her hand. "That's another thing about this job. You all don't know how to have a relationship. I'm glad I already found Harvey!"

"Is that all, Marvella?" Ernie asked from the door.

"That's all, sir. The sheriff and I have concluded our business. I'll be talking to you, Sheriff."

"Bye, Marvella."

Ernie gave Sharyn the Tylenol and another pill. "Echinacea and zinc. Trudy says take it. It'll work."

"Thanks." She swallowed both of them then sneezed again. Her head hurt and her throat was sore.

"I heard from Sheriff Two Rivers," Ernie told her. "Chavis is on his way back here. He was indicted to stand trial for shooting the sheriff and breaking out of jail but his trial won't come up for a month so we have all the time we need."

Sharyn explained everything she found out last night about the two separate incidents. "We don't have anything hard against Chavis for Monte's death. It's all circumstantial. But we've got plenty for Goodson."

The phone rang. It was the DA. "I hear that Montgomery Blackburn's death wasn't an accident after all, Sheriff. What are your plans?"

Sharyn sniffled while she explained about Chavis. "I don't know yet how we'll put the two together but I think they're related."

"I think we should issue an arrest warrant for both charges. Bring the man to justice, Sheriff."

"He'll be here later today for questioning, sir. If we find—"

"It sounds like you have him for both counts. What's your hesitation?"

"The case against Chavis for Monte's death is pretty bare, sir. We found those gambling tickets but that's all that links them.

"In this case, that's enough. Proceed against him."

She paused to wipe her nose. "Sir, with all due respect, I know you consider yourself to be the guardian angel of the Vets in this town but this is rushing the process some. Monte is dead. We'll find out what happened. But unless Chavis confesses—"

"Do you need someone else in your department to carry out the wishes of the DA's office, Sheriff? If I issue an arrest warrant from this office, I expect you to work with me."

"I think you're setting us up for a fall in court, sir. You of all people should know about rushing the process."

"I'll have those warrants sent down to you and we'll plan to arraign him today. Judge White is in session, I believe."

She put down the phone.

"What's up?"

"Percy wants to call both deaths murders. He wants to arraign Chavis for both of them later today."

Ernie took a sip of his coffee. "Well that's a fine kettle of fish."

"Yeah. You know how he feels about the Vets."

"I know. No other man in this town has done as much for them. Eldeon Percy is like the patron saint of veterans in Diamond Springs."

Sharyn coughed. "You sound like you admire him?"

"Being a Vet myself, I empathize with him. And I guess I admire him a little. He's done some good work. Look how he came down here in the middle of the night for Willy that time."

"We still can't let him make this happen without evidence. I don't like Chavis either. And I think maybe he suddenly got worse. But we need more to make this case. How about you and Cari going out and seeing what you can dig up? Did anyone ever see them together? Did anyone know about Monte placing bets with Chavis? Did he owe him money?"

"Okay. But I don't think you should be here by yourself."

"I'll be fine. Trudy's here to handle the phones. If something comes up, I'll call you. In the meantime, I'm going to send a picture of Monte up to Cherokee and see if anyone recognizes him."

"Sounds good, Sheriff. I'll let you know if I find anything."

Sharyn was working at her desk. Chief Wallace phoned in a report on the fire. It was down to the fire fighters up there making sure that the brush on the ground was out cold. All they needed was some rain to end it all.

Trudy buzzed her. "Don James here to see you, Sheriff, with Charlie Sommers."

Sharyn groaned. "Give me five minutes to shoot myself first, Trudy. Then send them in."

"You got it."

Don James was the publicist Sharyn's re-election committee hired to make her more acceptable to the public. She spent most of her time avoiding him. She wanted to win the election. She wasn't convinced a new hairstyle or makeup was going to make that happen.

"Sheriff!" Her PR man looked stricken when he saw her. "What's wrong with you?"

"I have a head cold."

"We'll have to call off the debate." Charlie Sommers took out his cell phone. He was the local head of the re-election committee for her party. "She's no match for Roy like this."

"It will be perceived as weakness if she backs down," Don James told him. "She's a woman in a man's job. She can't afford to be sick or tired."

Sharyn didn't remember the debate until they mentioned it. She was supposed to debate Roy at 6 P.M. at the old courthouse. "Maybe I'll be better by then."

Don glanced at Charlie. "Should we chance it?"

Charlie squared his shoulders beneath his tan wool jacket. "We don't have any choice."

"Let's get you to the doctor," Don said. "We can get you a shot of antibiotic and some zinc. Then we can take you to get makeup and clothes. It'll work."

"It will!"

Sharyn took a deep breath and tried to count but she kept sneezing. "I can't do that. Not right now anyway. We're expecting a prisoner from Cherokee that has to be inter-rogated. He might be arraigned later. I'll be at the debate. And I'll do my best. I don't think I need anything fancy to run rings around Roy."

"Don't underestimate him, Sheriff," Charlie warned. "He's good with a crowd."

"He's made you look bad a lot," Don explained like he was talking to a child. "And he's still ahead in the polls. Especially with older women and younger men."

"*What?*"

Don shrugged. "It's simple really. Older women see you not doing the traditional thing they did, marriage and ba-bies. Young men see you as a threat. Younger women see you as a role model. Older men are reminded of your father and what he stood for. Older women are less likely to vote than younger women. Younger men are more likely to vote than older men. There's a plus or minus of three points."

Sharyn felt like his explanation clogged up what little was left open of her sinuses. "I don't know about all of that, Don. But I know that I can hold my own against Roy Tarnower. With or without a cold. But I have business that has to be taken care of today. If I don't do my job as sheriff, there won't be a plus three points at all."

Don glanced at Charlie. "We'll have to chance it."

Charlie nodded. "We're depending on you, Sheriff. We need you to come through for us. Especially after this mess with Caison."

"This is the wild card race," Don told her for the hundredth time this month. "Anything could happen."

"What about Senator Talbot and Jack Winter?"

"Jack is an independent now," Charlie told her. "Our party nominated Caison. What happened to him was unfortunate. But we're standing behind him."

"To the grave," Don pronounced dramatically while he was examining his cuticles.

"Whatever." Charlie shook Sharyn's hand. "We'll meet you there tonight. Good luck."

"And wear something dark. Your red hair makes you look flighty." Don waved goodbye.

Sharyn sighed and let her head drop down on the desk after they were gone. Just what she needed, a big debate with Roy.

Ernie and Cari came back to the office a short time later.

"I saw the sheriff's car with Chavis pulling into the lot on our way in," Cari told her.

"Good. It's been so quiet I almost fell asleep," Sharyn answered. "What did you find out?"

Ernie shook his head. "It was pretty easy. Chavis has rousted Monte a few times. Beat him up pretty good at the beginning of the year. Monte spent his pension on medicine instead of paying Chavis."

Sharyn sat back in her chair. "So he was a regular?"

"Yep. All the guys down at the VA knew about it. Some of them put bets with Chavis too. They said he can get pretty rough if they can't pay."

"I guess we all knew that. Anybody actually see Monte get into the car with Chavis recently?"

"Nope. No help there, Sheriff."

She got up. "I guess we go with what we have."

Chavis wasn't in the building yet when Toby Fisher joined them. The assistant DA was carrying the arrest documents for the prisoner in his briefcase. "Sheriff Howard. How are you?"

"Mr. Fisher." She nodded back at him. "We're going to question Chavis before we arrest him."

Fisher glanced nervously at his watch. "Mr. Percy has his arraignment and bail hearing set at one o'clock. I hope we can make it fast."

Sharyn was more irritated than she needed to be. She left the assistant DA in the conference room before she said something she'd regret. She sneezed and coughed. Trudy made her some tea and gave her some cough drops. "I don't know why I feel this way. I think Chavis is guilty too."

Ernie laughed. "Because you don't like anybody telling you how to run your office?"

"I know. Just like my daddy."

"Yep."

"What's the point in questioning him if it all comes out the same way, Sheriff?" Cari asked standing beside her while the deputies from Cherokee brought in their prisoner.

"I don't know, Cari. But I'd like you to take notes, please."

"Sure thing." The deputy smiled at Toby Fisher.

The assistant DA smiled back at her through the open doorway and shifted his briefcase.

"In here, please." Ernie guided the deputies towards the interrogation room.

"Sheriff." Sam Two Rivers made the trip down with them. "Got a call from Bruce last night. He says things are quieting down."

"I think so."

"Bad cold?"

"Yeah."

Sam rubbed his hands together very quickly and held them against her face while he muttered something in Cherokee that she couldn't understand. "Try that. It should help."

"Thanks." She sniffed. Her head was vibrating but her sinuses felt better. She looked at Sam. He smiled and winked at her. It was probably the cough drops.

When Chavis was in the interrogation room, Sharyn and Ernie went in with Cari. The Cherokee deputies signed for the release of their prisoner then left him there with them.

"Mr. Whitley," Sharyn began when they were all seated, "I think you know why you're here."

"It's that stupid thing about that Goodson boy, right? I suppose you found all kinds of evidence that I killed him?"

"You could say that. Would you like to tell us about it?"

"About what? He placed some bets with me while he was here. Nothing spectacular. I went up to Cherokee. End of story."

Ernie shuffled his feet. "We found some evidence in the back of your Durango, Mr. Whitley. Blood and fingerprints from Mark Goodson. How did those get there?"

"Maybe he cut himself shaving and was looking for something in the back of my car. Who gave you permission to do that anyway?"

"We also searched your house and found gambling receipts from the same day that Mr. Goodson was at Harrah's gambling. A card dealer up there put the two of you together."

"Not together. Maybe we were there at the same time. That doesn't mean we were together."

"What about Montgomery Blackburn." Ernie shifted tactics.

"Who?"

"Monte who lived under the Clement's building."

"Oh, him? Was that his name? Yeah, I placed a few for

him every month. I place a few for a lot of people. Big names too. I could blow this whole town wide open."

"We found his body, covered in whiskey and set on fire in the back of a car that rolled down here from Center Street."

"And you think I killed him too?" He looked around at the faces of his accusers. "This is stupid. I'm not saying another word until I get a lawyer."

Toby Fisher got to his feet. "You don't have to have a lawyer until you're accused of something, Mr. Whitley. Let me remedy that situation. Chavis Whitley, you are being arrested for the murders of Montgomery Blackburn and Mark Goodson. The deputies will read you your rights. Then we'll be going over for your arraignment and bond hearing. I wouldn't expect to make bond if I were you."

Chavis squirmed in his handcuffs. "I want a lawyer now!"

Chapter Seven

Ernie and Cari accompanied the prisoner to the courthouse through the new annex. Sharyn turned to the assistant DA before he could leave. "Don't come into my office again like that."

"I'm sorry, Sheriff. Mr. Percy was very specific. I just do what I'm told. I don't want to make trouble for you. But I want to keep my job."

"I won't let my people or the law enforcement of this town be run over roughshod by you or Mr. Percy. I understand that you're only doing your job. Next time, let's work together."

"I'll do the best that I can." He adjusted his bright blue tie. "But you know that Mr. Percy calls the shots. Maybe someday that'll change. If I can hold on to my job."

She laughed. "Are you already stumping for my vote?"

Fisher blushed. "Maybe I am. Good luck on your re-election, Sheriff."

Trudy sighed as she watched him leave. "Well, what a surprise! He's a sweetheart."

"Or he just really wants to be the DA," Sharyn retorted.

"Either way. It's nice to have someone from that office who's decent to talk to."

"I know." Sharyn went to get a fax that was coming in. "This pretty much clinches it. The card dealer in Cherokee that can put Chavis with Goodman also recognized Monte

103

being with them. I guess I'm just being stubborn. The whole thing makes sense. I suppose I hate the way it went down."

"If you don't keep the DA in check, he'll get to be like old Jack Winter. We both know that!"

"Are we sure he's any different?"

"Ernie thinks well of Mr. Percy. Maybe you just don't feel good, huh? Why don't you go in your office and try to get some rest. I'll call you if there's an emergency."

Sharyn was willing to admit defeat, at least temporarily. "Thanks, Trudy."

"Don't worry, Sheriff. Things will work out. You'll see."

Sharyn stretched out in her father's old chair with her feet on the heavy desk. Pictures of all the sheriffs of Diamond Springs looked down at her, including her father's familiar smile and her grandfather's frightening scowl. They all had to deal with people like Percy and Winter. It wasn't only her. She studied her father's square-jawed face and vibrant eyes. *Unless you worked with them, Dad.*

The back door to the office slammed open against the wall.

Trudy cried out, "Ernie, what's wrong?"

He didn't answer as he raced into Sharyn's office. "He got away!"

Sharyn sat up. "Who?"

"Chavis!" Ernie exclaimed. "He was standing next to Cari and took her gun from her. There wasn't anything we could do but let him go."

"Did he take a car?"

"No," Ernie replied as he took a rifle from the storage locker. "He's holed up in the courthouse with Cari in one of the new courtrooms. No one else is in there. The security guards have him pinned down right now. But we gotta get her out of there!"

She saw that his head was bleeding. "You're hurt!"

"He clipped me with the gun when I tried to get it away from him. I was stupid to let her that close to him. This is my fault."

"Cari's a deputy too," she reminded him. "It could've happened to anyone."

"Yeah, well, he's not gonna do anything else." He loaded the rifle. "Grab yourself one, too, Sheriff. We might be able to pick him off through one of the windows in there."

"Have you tried talking to him?"

"What's there to say?" He wiped away the blood that trickled down the side of his face. "I think this rifle can say what needs to be said. Let's go!"

Sharyn wasn't so sure. "I think you should go to the hospital and let them look at that."

"There's no time for that now! Chavis is desperate. He might kill Cari. *It's my fault!*"

She put her hand on the rifle. "Ernie, go and let someone look at your head. I'll handle this. You're too upset to see straight right now. Joe and Ed are coming in to back me up."

"Sharyn, I will *not* go to the hospital until Cari is safe! You can fire me when it's over if you like. But I'm not leaving her there with him!"

Ernie was always so calm, so composed. Sharyn was hard pressed to know what to say to his dogged determination to get Cari out of there at all costs. She knew what it was like to feel responsible for someone. Didn't she kill the madman who hurt Kristie? "All right. Let's go. But leave that rifle here."

"Sheriff, I—"

"That's an order, Deputy! You leave it here or you go to the hospital. Take your pick!"

Faced with her steely-eyed demand, Ernie put down the rifle. "Let's go then. We're wasting time."

The courthouse was already buzzing with reporters and onlookers. They were drawn to the dangerous situation like flies to old meat. Television cameramen were setting up cameras while their reporters are setting up scenarios. Curious spectators who were at the courthouse snapped pictures of the scene. A young bride and groom in their wedding clothes watched in amazement. Courthouse security tried to push them away from the room where Chavis took Cari but the crowd pushed back.

Joe was there a minute after they arrived. He was wearing camouflage gear and sunglasses. With authority that the security guards lacked, he began to move the crowd away from the scene.

"Give him a hand until Ed gets here, huh?" Sharyn asked Ernie.

Ernie growled but did as she requested. She watched him go then laid her grandfather's gun on the polished green floor and went inside the unfinished courtroom.

"Sheriff!" Ernie yelled a second too late. He swore softly and hit the wall with his fist.

"I know you didn't think she was going to ask you to do it," Joe said. "You have to know her better than that by now."

"If somebody had to do it, it should've been me!"

"Maybe in another dimension! Let's get these people back before anyone else gets hurt. Man, you need to see a doctor."

"Never mind me." Ernie stared at the closed door and prayed.

"Chavis?"

"Go away!"

He was behind the new judge's desk. Sharyn knew the wood was thick and it made a good barrier. Ernie was right, there were two big windows flanking him. If they had to, they could try to get a clean shot from there. But Cari was too close to him, it could be bad for her.

"You know I'm not going to do that. Let the deputy go."

"No. What's the point? This case is all sewed up nice and neat. Nobody wants to hear what I have to say."

"I do."

"You just want to get your deputy away." He laughed. "She's a cute little thing, Sheriff. But you shouldn't trust her with a gun."

"Can she talk for herself?" Sharyn asked him. "Cari? Are you all right?"

"I'm fine, Sheriff." Cari answered in a frightened voice.

"Good. Then no damage has been done, Chavis. Let her go."

"No! I want a car and some cash. I want a cleared road out of the county. Then I'll turn her loose."

"You'd be picked off the minute you left this building," she bluffed. "Let the deputy go. Surrender your gun."

"You're not getting it, Sheriff. I'm dead no matter what happens. If somebody doesn't shoot me now, I'll rot in prison until I get the death penalty for something I didn't do."

"You have a trial to tell your side. Even if you're convicted, you can appeal. That's how the system works. You know that." She looked for other ways around the huge bench and pedestal that hid him from her.

"Who's gonna believe me? I've been in jail. Everybody knows about me. I won't get a fair trial. Everybody wants to believe I killed Goodson and Monte."

"Tell me your story," she urged. "I promise to investigate whatever you tell me."

"I'm not playing games with you. I've been here before. I got nothing to lose. Get me a car and some cash. Let me go. I swear I'll do right by the deputy. I don't want to hurt her. I don't want to hurt anybody."

"Take me," Sharyn suggested. "Take me instead of Cari. If you have me with you, nobody will try to shoot you. I'm the sheriff. She's just a deputy. Let her go and I'll get you the cash and a car."

Chavis was silent while he considered her offer.

"I'm calling out right now." Sharyn pushed him. "How much cash do you think you need?"

"How much do you have?"

"We've got about fifteen hundred in petty cash at the sheriff's office. I can lay my hands on that right away. It can be here in five minutes."

"Okay," Chavis agreed. "I'll swap you for her."

"We'll take my Jeep," she said, speed dialing Joe's cell phone.

"What's going on?" Ernie demanded when Joe was on the phone with Sharyn. "Why didn't she call *me*?"

Joe nodded and closed his cell phone. "Maybe because you're freaking her out! She's coming out with Chavis. She wants us to get the petty cash from the office and her Jeep and take them to the back door."

"No way!" Ernie countered angrily. "She's not coming out with him like *that!*"

"Calm down, Ernie." Ed arrived and put his hand on his friend's arm. "She knows what she's doing."

Ernie threw his hand off. "You don't get it! It's my fault Cari is in there! If he takes Sharyn . . . I won't let that happen!"

Joe stopped him. "Ernie, we've been friends and worked together for twenty years. I'm telling you, man, you have to back down here. Sheriff says this is the way we're gonna play it. They pay her to make those decisions, remember?"

"You stay here," Ed said to Ernie with a glance at Joe. "I'll go and get the cash and the Jeep. The sheriff can take this guy out. She just needs the right chance."

Chavis peeked around the corner of the judge's bench. Sharyn held up her hands to show him that she wasn't carrying a weapon.

"Throw me your cell phone," he ordered, standing up. He brought Cari up against his chest.

"Don't do this, Sheriff. I'll go with him," Cari volunteered as tears slid down her face.

"Who wants *you*?" Chavis shoved her to the floor. He held the gun on her while he beckoned to Sharyn, "Come on, Sheriff. We're gonna get real close here."

Sharyn slid her cell phone along the dusty new floor. She hoped Cari would respond to her signal and they could take the man out before it went any further. But Cari lay on the floor, whimpering. She was too terrified to look up.

"Come on, come on! We ain't got all day, Sheriff!"

She went to him with her hands in the air. He turned the gun on her, pressing it into her chest. Then he had her wrap her arms around his neck so they could walk out cheek-to-cheek.

"Just pretend I'm your lover." He laughed. "You're too tall for a woman, you know that?"

Sharyn did as she was told. Chavis smelled like sweat and worse. With the gun against her heart, she didn't dare make a move against him. She would have to go with him to the Jeep then work on a plan. At least Cari was safe.

It was hard to surrender that way. She didn't realize how hard it would be to push aside all of her instincts to run or fight. Everything inside of her wanted her to make a move. Her heart was pounding. Her brain was working overtime. But she was calm and clear headed. She knew she could get the gun from him in the car and do whatever was necessary.

"Okay! I'm coming out with the sheriff," Chavis yelled. "We're going out the back door through the new way. That Jeep and cash better be there."

Sharyn saw Nick's face in the crowd. She wanted to reassure him that it would be all right. He started forward and Ed held him back with his hand against his shoulder. Chavis kept his back to the smooth wall. The gun dug deeper into Sharyn's chest. Video cameras picked up the whole thing. The bride and groom wasted their wedding film on the escape. Camera flashes burst in their faces.

Ernie drew his gun. Joe snatched it from him. "What are you doing?"

"We won't get a better shot."

"Did you see how his hand was shaking? Did you see where he was holding that gun on her? He'd squeeze off a round if somebody sneezed! She wouldn't live through it. We've got to let them go!"

It was a slow moving tableau for Sharyn as they walked down the long hall to the annex. She saw Ed and Nick following them. Joe and Ernie ran into the courtroom they left.

"Back off!" Chavis yelled at Ed then shoved the gun deeper between Sharyn's breasts. "Tell them! This was your idea!"

The cold metal bit at her flesh. Sharyn took a deep breath. "Ed, Nick, back off. I promised Chavis he could have the money and the Jeep and take me along to the county line if he let Cari go."

Ed nodded. "Right, Sheriff."

Nick kept going until Ed pulled him back. Sharyn saw Ernie, Cari and Joe's faces before they turned the corner into the new construction.

"We're not letting him take her, right?" Nick demanded when they couldn't see them anymore.

"Of course not," Ed declared. "We've got the highway patrol standing by on the interstate. If we can't catch them ourselves they'll get them. Let's move!"

Cari stayed with Trudy at the office. David and JP rolled past Ed and Joe, leaving the impound lot ahead of them. Ernie and Nick scrambled for a car.

Ernie barely noticed Nick until they were on the road. "Why are you here?"

"Why do you think? Can't we go any faster?"

"Yeah, when we find them."

"We've got 'em," David reported over the radio. "Headed south on Center towards the Interstate."

Ernie jerked the car towards the directions. "You shouldn't be here. This isn't a good time to get emotional."

"Shut up and drive, Ernie!"

"Go faster," Chavis urged her, poking the gun in her side from the passenger's seat. He looked back along the road. Two sheriffs' cars were behind them.

Sharyn knew it was lucky that Chavis couldn't drive a stick and he had to let her drive. That was a plus in her favor. She couldn't do much with the gun in her heart and him pressed against her like a piece of taffy. The car was different. She needed to divert him. "Why don't you tell me what happened? Maybe I can still help you."

"You've helped already, Sheriff." He looked at the money as he stashed it in his pockets.

"You said you didn't kill Goodson or Monte."

"I didn't. I took Monte up to Harrah's with me. He wanted to go. I thought I was doing him a favor. A friend asked me to help Goodson while he was down here. I loaned him some cash to gamble with at the casino. That's it."

"Then what happened?"

"Drive faster!"

She put her foot down harder on the gas pedal. "Then what happened?"

"We came back here. He lost big time. Goodson told me he had the money to pay me back. He didn't. My friend said he was good for it but he was wrong. I had to teach him a lesson. I told him there was a big game and went to pick him up. I took him up on the mountain and roughed him up a little."

"You beat him pretty good according to the autopsy."

"Whatever! The point is that he was still alive when I left him up there! I figured the walk back would clear his brain a little. Maybe keep him from being so stupid. But I didn't kill him!"

She held the car steady on the road as they approached the Interstate. She wasn't going to go that far with him. Being on the open highway driving faster would only make it worse. "What about Monte? Did he see you?"

"No. He wasn't anywhere around. I dropped him off after we came back from Harrah's. I didn't see him again. He knew better than to say anything anyway. Me and him were friends."

"Is that why you beat him a few times too?"

Chavis shrugged. "I did what I had to do. If I let him buy medicine with money he owed me, I'd have to let them all do it. I beat him up a few times. But I didn't kill him either! Not that it matters now. Drive faster! We're almost to the highway."

Sharyn knew where she was going. There was a truck roll up off the steep downhill ramp that led to the highway. When she heard the gravel crunch under her tires, she jerked the wheel to the right. Chavis was off balance for a moment as he fell back against the door. She slapped the gun out of his hand.

He kicked at her and she lost control of the Jeep. She fought to regain the steering wheel while the vehicle swung back and forth across the ramp. On either side was a drop of at least twenty feet. At the base were sand pits meant to help fight fires if a truck lost control on the incline.

Sharyn put her foot down hard on the brake and brought up the hand break at the same time. The Jeep jerked and the brakes smoked. The acrid smell was choking. Chavis wasn't strapped in and he flew against the windshield. He hit hard but bounced back at her, taking a wild swing at her face.

She ducked then fought to unlock her seatbelt and grab the gun he dropped on the floor. The Jeep teetered precariously at the edge of the ramp. She managed to get the belt unlocked and open the door. The gun was slightly out of reach. Chavis launched himself at her. They fell out of the Jeep together, rolling down to the bottom of the sand pit.

Chavis punched her in the side and Sharyn brought her knee up into his groin. The gun clattered down from the Jeep beside them. Chavis tried to kick her out of the way to reach it. She got there first. He put his hand over hers to wrestle it away and she bit him hard.

There was a loud retort that echoed off the tall pines away from the cars that raced by on the Interstate. Chavis looked surprised at first then he fell back in the sand with a growing red stain on his chest. Sharyn looked up to see Ernie standing over them on the ramp with his gun drawn.

Ed and Nick scrambled down to where Chavis fell while Joe called for an ambulance. Sharyn looked up at Ernie.

His eyes were hard and glassy as he stared at Chavis. He holstered his gun then turned away.

Joe picked up her gun and cleaned it off. "It was loaded, right?"

"Yeah. Thanks."

"Then it was a righteous shoot. I mean, there was no way to tell which one of you got the gun. And Chavis would've shot you if he got it."

"Yeah."

"Are you all right?" Nick reached her, stopping short of putting his arms around her.

"Just a little mangled. Nothing serious. What about Chavis?"

Ed shook his head. "He's gone." He handed Sharyn a handkerchief.

"Thanks." She dabbed the blood from her mouth. She could feel sand scratching inside her uniform and shoes. "Check on Ernie, huh?"

David almost fell down the embankment in his haste to reach her. "I hope he's dead!"

"He is," Nick told him.

"Did you shoot him?" David turned to Sharyn.

"No. Ernie did it."

He nodded. "Can you get back up the hill or do you want me to carry you?"

Nick's mouth tightened. He kept from hitting David by walking past them to the top of the ramp.

"I can walk, David. Help them with the body."

The sky above them grew dark. Thick clouds swirled and threatened.

"Maybe we'll get some rain," JP said, looking upward.

"Let's hope so," Sharyn agreed then she forced her aching body to climb up the sand and gravel to her Jeep.

Sharyn and Ernie waited at the crowded hospital together. Being with the sheriff's department didn't guarantee them speedy treatment right now. Their wounds weren't bad enough to come before people who couldn't breathe.

Even through the thick walls, they could hear the thunder rumbling. It shook the floors and rattled the windows.

"I don't hear any rain," Sharyn remarked when the silence between them became too much.

"This kind of storm doesn't bring rain," Ernie told her, still holding a thick bandage to his head. "Just some thunder and lightning. Maybe some high winds."

"That's just what they need up on the mountain."

"Sharyn—"

"You don't have to say it, Ernie."

"I want to say it, if that's okay."

She looked at him as she held an ice pack to her mouth. "If it makes you feel better."

"I'm sorry. I was way out of line. I saw red back there. It was my responsibility. I shouldn't have let Cari that close to him. I didn't think."

"She's a trained deputy. I sent her with you. It should've been fine. It wasn't. You know things happen sometimes."

"I know. But I wouldn't blame you if you asked for my badge."

She laughed. Then groaned when it hurt her mouth. "Ernie, you might quit if Roy wins but as long as I'm sheriff, I need you. You know there'll be an inquiry into the shooting. But we were all there."

He hung his head. "I know."

"But I'm not putting you on desk duty. I need your help investigating this thing with Chavis."

"What do you mean?"

"I mean that he denied that he killed either man. Since it was like his deathbed testimony, I'm sworn to investigate it."

"He was a low-life worm, Sheriff! I hate to warrant a suspension again but there's nothing to investigate. You know we're better off with him not on the streets anymore. He was scum!"

"But he might not have killed Monte or Mark Goodson. He didn't deny that he was scum. He did deny killing the two men."

Ernie shook his head. "If that don't beat all!"

"I don't want anyone else to know," she confided in him. "Not until we see if there's any evidence in his favor."

"The man was a liar! He would've said anything to get away with it!"

"Are you going to help me or not?"

He considered her request. "I guess if you're sworn to investigate, I'm sworn to help you."

"Good."

"But I think you're wrong."

"I don't care."

"I know."

She looked up as they were joined by two doctors. "Do you think Cari will quit?"

He shrugged. "I don't know. I gave up thinking a few minutes ago when I said I'd help you. My brain got fried at that point."

"Sheriff." Dr. Elizabeth Anderson studied her face. "I don't know how you do these things to yourself!"

"I don't know either, ma'am."

"It comes from plain pig-headedness," Ernie told her as his doctor took him out of the room.

Dr. Anderson smiled. "Well, let's get you cleaned up and see if there's any serious injury."

An hour later, with a clean bill of health, Sharyn was out of the hospital. The combination of smoke and heavy clouds made the afternoon dark. Streetlights tried to pierce the shroud but the light bounced back. Thunder continued to shake the ground. Lightning joined it, cracking against the sky.

"I take it everything is still where it belongs?" Nick joined her in the parking lot.

"Yeah. For now."

"How do you feel?"

"Sore and tired and sandy. Do you know what happened to my Jeep?"

"They towed it to the garage. Something about pulling up the parking brake going sixty miles an hour and the windshield resting on the hood. They thought you might not want to drive it."

"Guess I'll hike back to the office then. Or you could offer me a ride if your car is here."

"I think you're home for R&R the rest of the day," he told her. "This wind whipped up the fires on the mountain again. Trudy and Cari are at the office. Everybody else is up there except for Ernie. Annie took him home a few minutes ago."

She held her head up to look him in the eyes. "Which is why you're here? To make sure I get home safely?"

"That's it. And to return this." He handed her gun to her. "I don't want to tell you how I maneuvered to be here. The reporters are on the other side of the hospital. I thought it was safe."

"Thanks." Her holster was ripped during the fight. She tucked it into the back of her dirty, sandy uniform pants. "I don't want to go back to the office anyway."

He rested his hand on her forehead. "You don't feel like you have a fever. But I know something must be wrong with you."

She smiled and shook her head. "Nothing that a hot bath and a good night's sleep won't help."

"Then let's go." He opened up the door to the vehicle beside them. It was a huge, black Cadillac SUV.

"Wow! Yours?"

"Yeah. I like your Jeep a lot. But I wanted something with more room. Like it?"

"It's big. They must pay you better than they pay me."

"Yeah. I get all the perks." He closed the door behind her and got in on the driver's side.

Sharyn watched the jagged lightning illuminate the unnaturally dark sky. "I'm getting afraid to look up at the mountain. I'm afraid I'm going to see that fire coming straight for us."

"You'd think we could get some rain with all this thunder and lightning." He chided himself for talking about the weather. It was worse than talking about the job. But he didn't have any smart answers to reassure her.

"You'd think."

"This lightning could start a whole new fire."

"Yeah. Just what we need."

They both sighed at the same time and gave up the fight. Conversation was impossible.

The roads were strangely deserted for that time of day. Sharyn looked at the fires raging again on their side of the mountain. The threat of evacuation glared at her with the angry orange lights. "Do you think the people of Pompeii felt this way? Did the sheriff there wonder how she was going to get so many people out of the way if the fires came racing down the mountain?"

"I'm sure if the sheriff of Pompeii wasn't beaten up and exhausted, she'd know she'd find a way to work it out."

"Maybe."

Nick drove as slowly as he could but the time was over quickly. There was never enough time. He pulled the big SUV smoothly into her drive. He kept his hands on the steering wheel and let the engine run. He'd be less likely to do something stupid that way. For all of his good intentions, he was blind and helpless when he was with her.

Sharyn knew she should open the door, thank him for the ride, then go inside. Instead she sat there, watching the fierce lightning slash at the mountain that loomed over Diamond Springs. She made excuses for herself. *She was sore and tired. She needed a few minutes to get out of the car. If he didn't throw her out, she'd get out in another minute.*

"This is stupid," Nick said finally.

"I know."

He turned to face her and dared to take his hands off the steering wheel. "So what do we do about it?"

She looked at his face hungrily. "I don't know. I have to tell you something. I lied to you."

He frowned. "About what?"

"When I told you that I had a relationship for two weeks.

It was really only ten days. It was wrong of me to mislead you."

"Sharyn Howard!" He put up his hands in mock affront while he mimicked her southern drawl. "You cad!"

She laughed at him. "If you wore a uniform, people might think you were me."

He leaned towards her and kissed her lips gently, mindful of her sore lip. "We can work this out. It's less than a week now. I've already made reservations for the new production of Hamlet and dinner at the Regency Hotel. When people see us together for the first time, we'll be out in style."

"That sounds great." She sighed, happy that she was close to him. "Maybe we can keep people from killing each other that night."

"Maybe." He kissed her forehead. "If they do, we'll ignore them."

Sharyn's mother leaned her head out of the door. "Sharyn? Nick? Is that you out there?"

Sharyn took Nick's hand. "Come in for a while. I don't see any video cameras around."

He kissed her fingers. "Okay. But only if I can fall asleep on your floor watching TV."

Sharyn laughed and climbed carefully out of the SUV behind him. Hand-in-hand, they walked towards her house. A fork of lightning stabbed into the heart of Diamond Springs. An explosion followed that rocked the ground beneath their feet.

Chapter Eight

Sharyn and Nick were on the scene as the first group of fire fighters arrived. The fire raged outside the Clement's building. There was too much black smoke to see what happened. Two more groups of fire fighters jumped down from their trucks and added their support.

Nick sniffed the air. "Gas and oil. It must be one of the pieces of equipment they're using out here."

"I'm surprised there are any fire fighters down here with the fire on the mountain coming back this way."

"You'd be surprised how organized they are so that it doesn't happen that way," he explained. "They know who's up there and who's down here. There's a lot of volunteers in this area too. It would be hard to catch them off guard."

"Sheriff." Chief Wallace nodded to her as he arrived in his white and red pickup. "What's going on out here?"

"We just got here," she told him. "We heard the explosion and followed the black smoke this way. Nick thinks it might be a piece of equipment."

"Smells that way. There's a lot of heat and the smoke is like pitch. You've got a good nose, professor!"

"Thanks. Need a hand?"

"I think we're covered. I saw you up on the mountain getting that boy out who was overcome by smoke. Good job!"

"I'm glad I was there to help," Nick replied gruffly with a glance at Sharyn.

"Could be lightning," the chief considered. "I hope nobody was in there." He put on his helmet and headed for the darkest area of smoke.

"So you're a hero, huh?" Sharyn teased Nick.

"This from a woman who leaves her gun in the hallway and offers to take her deputy's place as a hostage! How can I hope to compete?"

"I don't think we're competing. But I'm proud of you."

"Thanks. But next time, don't let the bad guy take you hostage. Okay?"

"Yeah. Right."

Another, smaller explosion made the fire flare up into the leaden sky. Nick took Sharyn's arm and moved away from the intense heat with her in tow. "We're too close."

The fire was fueled by the high wind, incinerating dry leaves and paper it met in the air. Lightning continued to flash and stream through the sky. It wasn't safe for anyone to be out but the fire fighters stood their ground, pouring water on the blaze.

Cari drove up in a sheriff's car and joined them. The noise from the fire and the shouting of the crews made it impossible to talk so close to the building. They stepped back to the street as a second unit of fire fighters came to the scene.

"What happened?" Cari asked her, shielding her eyes as she looked at the fire.

"We don't know yet," Sharyn explained to her in a loud voice. "Any calls on it?"

"No. I heard the explosion and came over. Was anyone in there?"

"I don't know. The chief went to see what was happening."

"It doesn't seem like the crew would be working in this weather," Nick added "Hopefully they all went home."

"Anything I can do?" Cari asked. "I was told you were off duty for the rest of the day."

"I'm not here officially," Sharyn replied with a smile. "I'm nosy and I wanted to know what was going on down here."

Another small explosion shook the area, adding more fuel to the fire. A fire fighter walked slowly towards them through the smoke and flames, long streams of water shooting above her. Melinda removed her mask from her soot-covered face. "Nick, can you give me a hand? I'm at the point of origin. Fire's out there but I could use another critical eye."

"Let me suit up." He went back to his SUV without hesitation.

"What's happening in there?" Sharyn asked her. "What are the smaller explosions?"

"Chief thinks the backhoe was hit by lightning. Smaller explosions were a gas-powered chainsaw and something else we haven't figured out yet."

"What about people?" Cari pushed her way into the conversation.

Melinda glanced at her like she didn't notice her before. "No one was in there as far as we can tell. Crew went home for the day because of the weather."

Nick came back in a full yellow suit, holding his mask. "I'll follow you in."

Melinda nodded. "This way."

"Good luck." Sharyn realized how Nick felt when he saw her leaving the courthouse at gunpoint. It wasn't a pleasant experience.

"I should go on patrol. Unless you think they might need me here." Cari shrugged but didn't go back to her car.

"I think they can handle it. There's no traffic so we're okay there." Sharyn glanced at her. "Is something wrong?"

"I guess this isn't a good time to talk about it. But I'm really sorry for letting you down today. I don't know what happened to me. I was just so scared. I couldn't think or move. I was like a deer caught in the headlights. I guess you wouldn't know how that feels, huh?"

"Of course I know how that feels! Everyone goes through that sometimes. I'm afraid too. And the first time I saw a dead body, I threw up."

"You didn't?"

Sharyn nodded. "And everyone laughed at me. Joe and Ed teased me about it for weeks. No one knows how they're going to react in a situation until it happens. I think anyone would've been afraid in that situation, Cari. You don't have anything to apologize for. You didn't let me down."

"I let that man take my gun away."

"You're right. And I think you should be more careful next time. But so much of this job is experience. I learn something new every day. You learned from this experience. I guarantee you no one will take your gun away again."

Cari nodded. "You're right, Sheriff. Thanks. I told myself the same thing after it happened. I won't ever be that stupid again. Ernie said it was his fault. But I knew he was wrong."

"You're welcome. But don't think you won't ever make a mistake again. It happens. And Ernie feels responsible for everything that happens. That's the way he is."

"I guess. You were right about Ed, too. Ernie's a good man, isn't he?"

Sharyn swallowed hard. *Cari wouldn't think about Ernie as a replacement for Ed, would she?* "He's a good man and a good partner. I heard a little gossip that he and Annie are getting married later this year. Maybe Christmas."

"Really? I wasn't sure how close they were."

"They're tight. Ernie's been in love with her since they were in school together."

"Oh. That's great for them."

"Yeah."

Cari sighed. "Well, I'm going to patrol the lake area. If you need me, call."

"Thanks." Sharyn took a deep breath. She hoped Cari's brain wasn't working that way but she wanted to dig that root out before it could grow at all.

A few spectators came to watch the fire but most stayed indoors. Fire was becoming tedious in Diamond Springs.

The crew foreman walked up beside her. He was a short, sturdy man. His jeans were unzipped and his hair was wild on his head. He wiggled his bare feet in the water that raced down the street from the fire hoses. "What happened, Sheriff?"

"They think one of the pieces of equipment was hit by lightning."

"Lightning? Man, that will set this back for weeks."

"No crew left on the scene?"

"No, ma'am. I called it a day after that lightning started. I didn't think about lightning hitting anything except people."

"Sheriff?" Chief Wallace ran back to them. He glanced at the man beside her. "Are you the foreman?"

"Yeah. Jim Raymond."

Chief Wallace reamed the man about the gas-powered chainsaw and leaving the debris all over the work area. "Lucky for you, none of my people were injured. Anything else in there we should know about?"

The foreman shook his head. "There was no way for me to know this would happen."

"Maybe not but this was careless negligence. The county lets us charge anyone convicted of it with the full amount of the bill for having to come to the scene. I hope you've got a hefty checkbook, Mr. Raymond."

The foreman was speechless, staring at the blaze that might mean his future.

"There's something I think you should see." The chief put his hat and mask on Sharyn. "Keep your head down. That should help."

"Thanks, Chief." Sharyn nodded and followed him.

The fire was nearly extinguished as they walked into the area. It looked like a set from a war movie. Smoke was still heavy and dark but it was beginning to dissipate. Everything was drenched. The area affected by the fire was scorched. There was a big crater around what was left of the backhoe where the fire started. Fire fighters were working on the area, picking up pieces of debris and stacking them together. Sharyn nodded to Melinda and Nick as she came up to where they were working.

"The explosion wasn't caused by a lightning strike," Nick told her.

"The gas line to the backhoe was broken." Melinda showed her.

"Couldn't the explosion do that?" Sharyn asked her as she studied the thick line.

"No. See how smooth the edges are? The blast didn't do that. Probably wear."

"It's amazing it was still intact after the explosion," Nick explained.

"What?" Chief Wallace demanded, his voice harsh and dry with smoke. "What do you mean? It didn't spontaneously combust!"

"Nick?" Melinda let him explain.

"I'm sure you know about static, Chief. It's why they tell you not to use your cell phone at a gas pump. Gasoline can be ignited by static. With these dry lightning strikes, we think that's what happened."

"Somebody was darn lucky there wasn't a full crew out here when it happened! I've half a mind to press charges against that foreman!" The chief glared back at where the foreman had been on the street but the man was gone. "What about the building?"

"She was built to last," Melinda told him. "Very little damage."

"Too bad," Sharyn replied. "It would've saved the city some money tearing it down."

Melinda shrugged and went back to work. Nick told her that he was going and she thanked him for his help.

Sharyn gave the helmet and mask back to the chief. "Let me know if you decide to prosecute. I'll have someone come down in the morning to put up signs around the building. I think it might be a while before they get back to work on it again."

Nick and Sharyn walked out together. She sat in the SUV while he stripped off his gear and stowed it in the back. There were still some hot spots that the last crew was putting out. Most of the other fire fighters left the scene.

She thought about Monte. If he was still living under the building, he might have been killed or seriously injured tonight. It wasn't a blessing exactly since he was murdered in such a terrible way. She hoped he was good and drunk at the time and didn't realize what happened to him.

"Where are you?" Nick asked when he was in the driver's seat and she was still staring out the window.

"Oh. Sorry. I was thinking about Monte."

"Yeah." He started the engine. "It was like he was destined to die in fire. If he was here tonight, it might've been the same thing."

"Nick, I know you're going to hate this. Ernie hates it."

"Please don't tell me—"

"I think Chavis was innocent."

"The man wasn't innocent, Sharyn! He was scum!"

She explained about his confession in the car. "It could be called a deathbed confession."

"It could be called the man saying whatever he thought you wanted to hear."

"Why? Why would he bother?"

"Because he knew the chances were that he was going to be caught," Nick argued as he drove back to her house. "Because people lie. Who knows why?"

"I think he was telling the truth."

"That he beat Monte and Goodson but he didn't kill them? That he took Goodson up the mountain and left him there but he was still alive? How can you believe that?"

"I don't know."

"It's getting late. You've had a tough day. When you think about it tomorrow, you won't believe you questioned that Chavis killed these men."

She glanced at him. "Right."

He parked the SUV in her drive again. Faye Howard's car was gone. "Looks like Faye went out."

Sharyn sighed. "Yeah, she thinks she's in love with Jack Winter now. He might be worse than Caison. Of course, if I change my mind about Chavis, I might change my mind about Jack, too."

He turned to face her in the dim light. "Sharyn, I know you like to champion the underdog. I understand that about you. But there's no evidence to support that anyone else murdered those men. We found Goodson's blood in the back of the Durango. We found his fingerprints. There were carpet fibers from the Durango on Goodson's body. Chavis admitted that Goodson owed him money he couldn't pay back. He was leaving Diamond Springs. It sent Chavis off the deep end. The man admitted to you that he beat Monte for spending his gambling money on medicine. Murder isn't that much lower."

"I can't explain it. But what if Chavis was telling me the truth? What if he didn't kill Goodson and Monte? That would mean we were looking in the wrong direction and the killer is still out there."

He rested his forehead on the steering wheel. "I give up. What do you want me to do?"

"Check out Goodson's body one more time."

"His ex-wife is coming here to claim it early tomorrow morning."

"Can't you stall?"

"You mean lie?"

"Whatever. Just take one more look for any anomaly that doesn't fit the picture we painted of his death."

"If we could find the murder weapon, that might help."

"I don't know if that's possible."

"I don't know if this is possible, Sheriff," he complained. "What am I looking for again?"

"Anomalies. Something that doesn't fit."

"You mean anything that might mean that Chavis didn't kill him?"

She nodded. "I mean anything that doesn't fit the profile."

"Okay. I'll go in now. If I catch on fire during the night, you'll know it's because my brain was fried."

She laughed and leaned forward to kiss him. "Good night, Nick. Thanks."

He wrapped his arms around her. "I'm going in to work *again* tonight. I need more than that."

A few minutes later Sharyn looked up and noticed that more than her mind was in a fog. The windows were steamed over. She laughed. "I think I should go."

"Good night, Sharyn. I'll let you know if I find anything. Which I know I won't. But maybe I can convince you once and for all that Chavis was responsible."

"I hope so. Good night, Nick."

He waited until she was in the house to leave. She watched the headlights fade away down the road. The house was quiet and dark around her. Her head hurt and she was exhausted. But mostly she was sandy and her muscles were sore from the pounding Chavis gave her. Nick and Ernie were right. She didn't know how she could consider that Chavis was innocent of anything. She wasn't sure he wouldn't have killed her if he got the gun first. Or if Ernie wasn't there to make sure it didn't happen.

A righteous shooting, Joe called it. Her gun was loaded. Chavis looked like he'd kill her if he got it first. Ernie was protecting her. Maybe saving her life.

She filled the tub with hot water then lowered herself carefully into it. She closed her eyes and rested her head against the side of the tub, promising herself that she wouldn't fall asleep. She was going to burn a candle but the thought of more smoke and fire wasn't pleasant. Instead, she turned off the ceiling light and left on a nightlight.

She knew she was fortunate not to have killed many people in her short career. If she were a rookie cop in Chicago, she would've killed more. The few people she killed became part of her. Their faces might blur someday but not yet. She recalled each of them and the incident of their deaths in great detail. Some were righteous shootings. Some were accidents that happened when she was trying to save someone's life. There was only one that was questionable for her.

Ernie was very emotional about what happened to Cari. She knew he was bound to be worse when it happened to her. Maybe he could've shot Chavis in the leg or the arm instead of the chest. She felt sure he did the best he could. But would Chavis think of firing if her deputies surrounded him? Was there really nothing else to do but shoot him?

A small sound grabbed her attention. She didn't move right away, just laid back and listened. Someone was in the house with her. Her first instinct was to call out for her mother to identify herself. It was bound to be her mother. Only a fool would break into the sheriff's house and everyone knew where the sheriff of Diamond Springs lived.

She stifled that impulse. A tiny voice in her brain warned her away from that course of action. It was like those horror movies that she and Ernie were joking about. Call out so that the intruder knew exactly where you were. Carefully, she shifted her position in the tub so she was upright without the water splashing.

She didn't have her gun. *Of course she didn't have her gun.* She didn't sleep and bathe with it. She was the sheriff and it was part of her clothes as much as her pants and her shirt. But off duty, the gun sat holstered in her closet. It was there right now. She opened her eyes when she heard the floorboard squeak in the kitchen. She'd known about that board since she was in high school, trying to sneak out without her parents' permission. Her mother had a talent for avoiding that board because it bothered her but she didn't want to replace it.

The bathroom was dimly lit. The rest of the house was dark. She knew she locked the door when she came in but that didn't mean anything to someone who was serious about breaking in. Her Jeep wasn't home so she had an advantage of sorts. The intruder didn't know she was home.

Maybe that's why he was there. Maybe he thought the house was empty. Her heart pounded a little faster in her chest. She controlled her breathing and thought about what she told Cari about being afraid.

There was nothing to use as a weapon in the bathroom unless she counted the plumber's helper. How many people surprised thieves in their homes and found themselves on the wrong end of a gun? Normally she would've smiled at the picture in her mind of attacking a would-be thief dressed in a towel holding a plunger. Quietly, she climbed out of the tub and wrapped a towel around herself. If it came down to it, she wasn't going to worry about being naked. Her life might depend on it. As amusing as it might be, she picked up the plunger and moved towards the door. It was better than nothing.

The hallway was dark and silent. The bedrooms were at the back of the house. A thief would be heading for other rooms first, looking for stereo equipment, microwave, computer. If she could reach her bedroom, she could grab her gun. Her fingers itched for the cold metal of the revolver. More for the confidence and sense of family it brought to her. She thought about her grandfather, Jacob, when she held it. Even when she used it, he was with her then. Not just a memory, but a past sheriff who defended Diamond Springs.

She lived in that house all of her life. She knew every crack, every squeaky board, every nuance of light. Taking a deep breath and fighting panic at being caught in such a helpless position, she crept to her bedroom. Hers was the last at the end of the hall. Her sister's was beside it. Her mother and father's room was across the hall. Between them was a linen closet and this bathroom.

A streetlight shone in through the living room window in front. There wasn't much left of its gleam by the time it reached her room. Besides, she had dark curtains for the days she had to sleep. It meant her room was dark and silent. The closet door was still open from when she changed clothes and decided on a bath.

She stood in the doorway for a long time before she finally plunged towards it. Holding the towel to her chest with one hand, she reached out for her gun with the other. Cool and deadly, it felt good in her grip. She turned towards the door and it closed, shutting her into the closet. She heard the lock turn but there was a key on the inside. It was a remnant of her childhood fear of getting locked in the closet. Forgetting the towel and everything else but the need to know who was in her house, she turned the key and burst out of the closet.

The sound of footsteps going out of the house drew her attention. She ran towards the sound. The door was open but there was no sign of anyone. The door wasn't forced. Someone used a key to get inside. As far as she knew there were only a few people with access to a key. None of them would sneak out the door without speaking to her. Or creep inside when they thought no one was there.

She ran out into the night but there was no car in the drive or on the street. The sound of an engine starting further up the road might be the offender. She knew she couldn't reach it in time, especially in her towel and bare feet. She was careful with the doorknob in case there were prints. But the chances were that whoever was here was too smart to leave evidence behind.

On the other hand . . .

A tiny spot of light drew her from the kitchen, clicking on lights as she went through the house. There was a flashlight left on the file cabinet in her father's den. It was a penlight with no special markings. The cabinet was closed. The light puddled inconspicuously on the wall near the window that fronted the street. Sharyn picked it up with the edge of her towel and examined it closely. Maybe the door wouldn't have prints but the flashlight might. There was also a scent in the house that wasn't a perfume or cologne she recognized right away. It was tangy and sharp, too sweet. Suddenly, she *knew*.

* * *

The tiny penlight clattered across the elegant glass desktop. Jack Winter looked up slowly from the papers he was reading. "Sharyn, what a nice surprise! Would you like some hot chocolate? I didn't forget how much you like that."

She loomed over him in the dark study. "Aren't you even going to pretend that you don't know why I'm here?"

"You're here to return my flashlight. Thanks." He clicked off the light and stowed it in his desk drawer. "Is there anything else I can do for you?"

Carefully, she lowered her hands until both of her palms were resting on his desk. Her face was even with his. "What were you doing in my house?"

"I went to get a sweater for your mother. We were at the rally together and she was cold."

"And that's why you were in *my* room?"

"Was that *your* room?" He chuckled to himself. "No wonder I couldn't find what she wanted."

Sharyn was never so hard pressed to keep from hurting another human being in her life. She studied her adversary. He'd been playing a game with her since she became sheriff. His pale blue eyes were colder than Diamond Lake. They held secrets that made her shiver with rage and fear. "This flashlight was in my father's old den. I caught you there once before. What are you looking for?"

He sat back in his expensive handmade leather chair and stared at her across his pyramided fingers. "What do you think I'm looking for, Sharyn?"

"If I knew, I wouldn't have to ask you!"

His voice was a shrouded whisper of dead leaves and cobwebs. "You don't want to know, little girl. Go home now. Before you find out something you can't make better with your shiny badge and your granddaddy's gun."

She stood up to her full height. "One day, you'll push me too far. Is that what happened between you and my father? You pushed him too far. He turned on you. Were you responsible for his death?"

He shook his graying head. "We've been through this. If you listen to Caison, you're bound to get confused."

"Talbot isn't talking much lately after what you put him through."

"I?" He got to his feet and sauntered to a well-stocked bar. "I had nothing to do with the poor senator's problems. Might as well blame that on your dear mother."

"Leave her out of this!"

His smile made his high cheekbones sharper. "Everyone is fair game, Sharyn dear. You. Your mother. Your aunt. Your sister. Did you think it ended with one?"

She wasn't wearing her uniform. But her grandfather's revolver was tucked into the back of her jeans beneath her sweater. Somehow, it made her take a step back and force herself to breathe. That's how this man got his power, through intimidation and fear. She couldn't lower herself to his level. "That makes you fair game too, Jack. Whatever it is you're looking for in my house must not be there. You've looked enough. It must be important to you. But give it up. If I see you there again, I'll shoot first and ask questions later."

"Like your deputy today?"

She smiled. She didn't know how she did it. But she had the pleasure of seeing the smile fade from his evil face. "Don't underestimate me. I'm not my father."

He poured himself a glass of bourbon and took a sip. "No, you're not. I can't tell you how happy that makes me. You're good for me, Sharyn. Someday you'll see that I'm good for you, too."

"We all have to dream. In the meantime, stay away from me, my house and my family."

He sat back down at his desk and returned to his papers. "Yes, well I have work to do. I'm going to be senator, you know. You can let yourself out the same way you got in."

She tossed a key down on the desk beside the flashlight. "I thought you'd have better security. I took this from my mother's purse and let myself in. If you're going to be a senator, you should consider hiring better help."

Jack Winter looked up but she was already gone. He chuckled over their game and finished his bourbon. Then he buzzed his security staff and fired them all.

Sharyn met Ernie at the office door with a cup of coffee in the morning. She didn't go back home. The fact that Winter walked by her in the bathroom while she was in the tub made her want to retch. She decided during the long night that there was only one thing to do. She was going to have to get her own apartment. If her mother wouldn't take her advice about Jack, she couldn't help her. If there was something in the house he wanted that belonged to her father, she didn't know what it was and wasn't able to find it. Either way, he made her skin crawl. She had to make a change.

"What's up?" Ernie asked, taking his coffee from her. "You don't look bright eyed and bushy tailed this morning. Bad night?"

"You could say that."

"Want to talk about it?"

They went into her office and she told him about Winter being in her house again. She didn't tell him about breaking into the ex-DA's house. "There's something there. Or he thinks there's something there. I don't know which. But I can't live with it anymore."

"What will you do?"

"I'm going to move out. I'm way too old to live at home anyway. This is the kick in the pants that I needed to get out."

His eyes were worried. "Is your mama serious about Jack?"

"I don't know. I think she likes the idea that it makes Caison crazy. I think she still loves him but she's too proud to admit it because he lied to her."

"That's a mouthful of psychology for this hour of the morning."

"I know." She smiled. "Sorry."

"So, what are we up to today? It feels funny asking *you*

that. I heard on the way in that the fires are under control again."

"For now. Ed and Joe went home after midnight last night so they won't be in today unless there's an emergency. Cari and Trudy are here. I hope David and JP will be on normal duty tonight."

"Which frees me up to look into those two murders, right?" He pulled at the tuft of hair on his head.

"Right. I don't want anyone else to know yet. I need some hard evidence or I need to forget it."

"Sheriff, take my advice and forget it right now. How much more evidence do you need to convict a man?"

"I don't know, Ernie. I have Nick taking one last look at Goodson's body before his ex-wife shows up for it this morning." The phone rang. "Maybe this is it."

Chapter Nine

"Okay. You asked for an anomaly," Nick reminded Sharyn on the phone.

"You found something?"

"I found something that might be unusual. It doesn't clear Chavis. I noted it on the autopsy records but didn't think much of it."

"What is it?"

"Talcum powder."

Sharyn slumped. "No wonder you didn't say anything before. How is talcum powder an anomaly?"

"I picked up a thumb and two fingers with it. No prints. But it's the same type of talcum powder that doctors use before they put on their gloves. Whoever did it was wearing gloves. We already knew that. Goodson wasn't covered with it but the places where I found it would be more consistent with where someone would touch him to drag him. There were two spots on Monte that had the same thing. His ankle and his shoulder. Again, there were scraps of cloth left there. The powder was on the cloth. I couldn't find any of it on the skin."

"Are you sure about this?

"Yes. But I wouldn't get out my dancing shoes yet. This doesn't prove anything. There may be millions of people who use this same powder. It could even be medical personnel who handled him before me. The only reason I said anything is because of where it is on their bodies. It's unusual."

"Thanks, Nick. You're doing an autopsy on Chavis, right? You can check him for the same powder? Then we'll know if we have something."

"I'm going to sleep for a few hours. Then I'll do Chavis. He's not going anywhere. Unless we evacuate the town, don't wake me up, huh?"

"You got it." She hung up the phone and looked at Ernie thoughtfully.

"Oh, don't tell me he found something that clears Chavis! I don't believe it!"

"No. He found something unusual on Goodson and Monte. Talcum powder. But it doesn't clear Chavis. Not yet anyway."

"Talcum powder doesn't seem to be much, Sheriff," Ernie observed. "Even if he finds some on Chavis."

"I know—"

"But then you can have him check anybody else that touched them, right?"

Sharyn nodded. "That's the plan. If it turns out to be nothing, we forget it."

"Okay." He shrugged. "You're the sheriff."

Ernie and Cari went out on patrol and left Sharyn in the office. Don James and Charlie Sommers hurried in to tell her the good news. "You're ahead of Roy Tarnower in the polls!"

"Really? How did that happen?"

"Haven't you see the paper this morning?" Don held it out for her. There was a picture of her after she got back from Chavis holding her hostage. The headline read: 'Sheriff Howard Does It Again!'

"The article calls you a hero in the truest sense of the word. A real life role model for our children," Don stated proudly.

"Is that the same paper that said I was bad for Diamond Springs last week?" Sharyn questioned.

Charlie laughed. "I know. People are fickle. But this is

your big break! Now they postponed the debate last night because of what happened. It's never been postponed before, you know. When you get up there, people are going to be thinking of you as a hero. Sound like a hero and you can multiply this lead into the double digits!"

Sharyn forgot about the debate. She wished they hadn't done her any favors in rescheduling it. "Isn't it enough that I'm ahead in the polls now? Can't we leave it at that?"

"The debate would solidify your lead," Don argued. "Everything we've worked for is right here, right now, Sheriff. You can't throw that away."

"All right." She sighed. "What time?"

"Tonight. Five P.M. at the old courthouse."

Don smiled. "Could you wear the same uniform you were wearing with the blood and dirt on it?"

"It already went to the cleaners, sorry."

"Oh well."

"That doesn't matter," Charlie told her. "Just wear your uniform and your biggest smile. Those bruises on your face and your cut lip say it all. The people will respond. You could win this election yet!"

"I'll be there," she promised, more than a little amused by it. Yesterday, she couldn't do enough. Today she was a hero. Yesterday, Roy was ahead in the polls. Today she was ahead. She was going to be glad when the election was over.

When they left her, she started on the paperwork to close up the files for Chavis, Goodson and Monte Blackburn. She did everything but sign the papers then she tossed down the pen. Her head ached, and not from the head cold. Either Sam Two Rivers cured that or Chavis beat it out of her, she wasn't sure which. Her knuckles were sore and bruised from hitting him. With terrible clarity, she recalled the instant when she saw him reach for the gun before her. She didn't doubt at that moment that he meant to shoot her.

"Sheriff?" Trudy interrupted her thoughts.

"Yes?"

"Ernie called in a minute ago. Seems there was another explosion and fire."

"The Clement's building again?"

"Nope. This time he's out on Old Pasture Road in one of those new subdivisions. He said it was Reed Harker's place."

Sharyn grabbed her hat and the keys for a sheriff's car. "I'm going out there, Trudy. Forward any calls to me."

"You got it."

Most of the 'new' subdivisions had been there for a few years. People from Diamond Springs still saw the people who moved there as the new folks. They weren't integrated into Diamond Springs culture. Most of them came from the big cities, Raleigh and Charlotte. They were looking for a better life and better schools for their kids.

But the growth cycle made Sharyn's position as sheriff unique compared to her father and grandfather. She was the first woman elected sheriff in North Carolina's history. She received praise for that. And she was watched because of it. Life changed for the sleepy little community in the past few years since she took office. Some people couldn't separate the difference between her being sheriff and the higher crime rate caused by the influx of new people.

She resigned herself to accept whatever happened in the coming election. Either people would elect her in for four more years or she would go back and take her bar exam. She dropped out of law school after her father's death. She knew she could always go back. Maybe she could make as much impact as a lawyer as she did as a sheriff. It was important to her that her life mattered. Her father and grandfather showed her that.

She called back to the office to ask Trudy to get an estimate on her Jeep being repaired. She didn't mind the patrol car but she missed her Jeep. It was actually her own car, not paid for by the city or county. They let her add it to the sheriff's insurance package so it was covered for things like high-speed chases and Chavis flying into the front window. But it was her baby.

She tried to put Chavis out of her mind. Maybe she was wrong about him. Even with Nick's discovery of the talcum powder, there wasn't enough there to shake a stick at, as her father used to say. When she thought back to those moments in the Jeep before he was killed, Chavis seemed sincere to her. If he'd lived, she would've continued to check into his story. They weren't given enough time to question him properly before he was taken off to be arraigned. She blamed herself for that.

Maybe that's what bothered her the most. Since he was dead, it was easy to tie up the whole package and put it in a file. She knew DA Percy wasn't going to like it. One of his Vets was dead. He wanted an answer. Chavis was it, nice and neat.

For now, she had to put it on the back burner. There were more pressing things happening. Any further investigation into the case would hinge on what Nick found out about the talcum powder. Even then she didn't know where to start. Besides, Chavis and gambling, there didn't seem to be any connection between the two dead men.

By the time she got out to the Courtly Lane subdivision, it was almost all over. The fire crews were packing up to go. She nodded to the weary eyed men and women who were working almost nonstop. It was bad enough that the fires on the mountain kept them working in rotating shifts around the clock. They didn't need the extra fires in the rest of the county.

"What happened?" she asked Ernie and Cari when she reached them.

"Chief said it was a natural gas leak in the kitchen. Lucky the family wasn't at home. They went out of town unexpectedly because Ms. Harker's mother got sick. Otherwise—" Ernie left the threat hanging.

Sharyn glanced up at the badly demolished brick home. Most of the back was still intact but the front was wet ashes and a pile of rubble. "Nice surprise to come home to."

"The chief said it was an accident. He said he's surprised

more of these houses don't go up since they slap them
together," Cari told her. "I guess we write it up as that."

"I guess so."

"Besides the fires on the mountain," Ernie counted, "that
makes two explosions and three fires in less than a week.
That must be some kind of record for the area."

"Like having floods when it rains," Cari added, trying to
help. "My mama always said, when it rains it pours."

Ernie grinned. "Like the little girl on the saltbox."

"I'm going back to the office. File your reports and I'll
notify the Harkers," Sharyn told them.

"Yes, ma'am."

Sharyn looked at the house again and her eyes narrowed.
"Ernie, does any of this seem strange to you? Maybe like
a pattern?"

"No, ma'am. It seems like some bad luck to me."

"We'll talk about it when you get back," Sharyn promised before she got in her car.

"I know we will." He held a hand to his head. "I need
to retire."

Cari was sympathetic. "What's wrong?"

"Let's finish the patrol and get to those reports, young
'un," he answered her. "I need to get back to the office and
put out the fire in the sheriff's brain!"

Sharyn was only a few minutes from her Aunt Selma's
farm. She had to cross six different places where they were
building the Interstate around it. But the old homestead that
had been in the Howard family for over two hundred years
was safe. It took some legal maneuvering to secure it but
Selma and Sharyn had it declared an historic landmark. The
house and land were held in a trust now.

Selma was out in back with a group of tourists who came
to buy her honey and look at her birds. Sharyn's younger
sister, Kristie, met her at the front door.

"Hi Sharyn."

"Hi. How are you?"

"Okay. Did Mom tell you I'm thinking of going back to school?"

"Yeah. That's great."

They sat together on the porch swing. The cool breezes blew most of the smoke and ash down towards Diamond Springs. It was remarkably unaffected out here.

"I'm sorry about everything that happened, Sharyn. I was a jerk." Kristie's blue eyes were filled with remorse. After being attacked by a madman the year before, she had dropped out of college and been picked up for shoplifting at the local mall.

"You weren't a jerk," her sister assured her. "You were hurt and confused. I wish I could've helped you more."

"You did the best you could. You have a whole county full of people who need you. I didn't mean those things I said to you about you being perfect and all."

Sharyn hugged Kristie. "None of those other people are as important to me as you. And I've already forgotten whatever you said."

"Thanks."

"I heard about Ernie shooting that dude," Kristie said, looking out over the old oak trees that surrounded the house. "I thought about what you said to me about what happened that day at the river when that crazy man had me. How you weren't sure if you could've avoided shooting? I think you did the right thing. I guess I would since you saved my life. I just wanted you to know."

Sharyn blinked away the tears that sprang to her eyes. She didn't trust her voice to speak so she sat next to Kristie and they kept the swing going in a slow, gentle rhythm.

Selma saw the sheriff's and walked over to the porch as her guests were leaving. "Hello stranger! Got some time for some apple cider?"

"Yes, ma'am." Sharyn got to her feet. "I was surprised to find you home instead of protesting the demolition of the Clement's building. I heard there was supposed to be another protest today."

"Oh, that." Selma waved her hand. "I was doing it for a

friend. Mary Jane Wagner? Her husband was one of the people who died there in the fire. It was so sad. Most of the protesters lost someone there. What could you expect them to do?"

Sharyn shrugged. "I don't know, Aunt Selma. You don't think they had anything to do with that backhoe blowing up, do you?"

"I thought that was an accident?"

"It was, according to the fire department. I was wondering what you thought. Emotions are running pretty high about that building right now."

"You know there's no accounting for what people would do, Sharyn," her aunt reminded her. "But even if they did, how could they do it and make it look like an accident? That would take some talent."

"You're right." Sharyn glanced around the homestead, admiring the late orange mums and bee balms. "Frost is coming late this year, huh?"

"I know. It's wonderful. Everything is so green. But it will come. It always does. Let's have the cider out here, huh?"

Selma Howard was the matriarch of her family. She took care of her parents in this house until they died. She went to her brother's funeral and held her niece's hand as she stood beside his grave. She and Sharyn were so much alike from their curly hair to the set of their jaws. Selma's once copper-colored hair was getting grayer every year but her blue eyes were sharp. She was tall and strong like Sharyn and had a will that didn't allow for anything to stand in her way.

After they were enjoying their cider and ginger cookies on the porch for a few minutes, Sharyn told her aunt about the visit from Jack Winter.

Selma shook her head as she bit down into a cookie. "That man can't ever leave well enough alone."

Sharyn sipped her cool cider. "I broke into his house and threatened him."

"You did what?" Selma and Kristie asked together. They laughed about it.

"You two have spent too much time together." She laughed with them. "I know it was wrong."

"It was stupid! That's the kind of thing he wants to have against you. He can control and manipulate people who do stupid things to get at him. I know you understand that."

"I can't believe you did something against the law." Kristie was in awe. "I didn't think you ever did anything wrong!"

Sharyn smiled as she took another cookie. "He threatened all of us. You, Mom, Kristie. Maybe it will be just as well if he wins that election and goes away for most of the year."

"Hush your mouth!" Selma warned. "The devil has ears, you know! That man should never have any power. He knows too well what to do with it."

"Are you going to turn yourself in now?" Kristie asked her sister.

Sharyn shook her head. "I don't think so. And if he wants to try to use it against me, he's welcome! I didn't do anything more than he did."

"That's the point," Selma assured her. "He draws you in and you don't realize what's happening. T. Raymond—"

"What about Dad?" Sharyn asked her when she stopped.

Selma bit her lip. "Nothing. I'm just a stupid old woman rambling on. Jack is dangerous, Sharyn. Don't let him own you."

"Aunt Selma, what about Dad? If there's something I should know—"

"You'd know it already. Some things should be buried with the dead." Selma stood up. "I have more visitors."

Sharyn followed her aunt, leaving Kristie on the porch. "Aunt Selma, did Winter have something on Dad? Did Dad do some of his dirty work? Is that what he's looking for in the house?"

"Even if I knew the answers to those questions, I wouldn't tell you. Ask your father, Sharyn."

"He's dead."

"My point exactly," Selma retorted cryptically. "Stay alive. And stay away from Jack Winter!"

Selma wouldn't say anything more. Her visitors kept Sharyn at bay. She watched her aunt playing the gracious hostess. Why wouldn't she tell her what happened between her father and Jack?

"She's pretty stubborn," Kristie observed, joining her.

"Yeah."

"Like my sister."

"You think so?"

Kristie laughed. "I *know* so! Want me to talk to Aunt Selma? Maybe I can wheedle something out of her that you can't get from direct confrontation."

She considered the offer. But she didn't know if Kristie should be involved. "I'll come back and drag it out of her. Don't worry about it. When are you thinking about going back to school?"

"Winter quarter in January. I think I can handle it now."

Sharyn hugged her again. "I *know* so!"

Ernie was waiting for her back at the office. "Sure. Drop a bomb on me and then run off to Selma's."

"What bomb?" she asked, hanging up her gun.

"I know you, Sheriff. I know your little brain is busy putting two and two together and coming up with a pain in my posterior section."

She closed the door to her office as they went inside. "You know me pretty well."

Cari started to get up and follow them then sat back down when the door closed. "Why do they do that?"

Trudy looked at the door. "Because they have things to discuss that they don't want everyone to know about. This office has a time keeping secrets from leaking out."

"I wouldn't tell anyone." Cari pouted.

"I'm sure you wouldn't. Go on and knock on the door. Tell the sheriff how you feel."

Cari did as Trudy goaded her. She knocked on the office door and stuck her chin out in defiance.

"Something wrong?" Ernie asked around the corner of the door.

"I want to be included in whatever you're doing," she told him. "I can keep a secret."

He glanced at Sharyn. She nodded and he stepped aside to let Cari into the office.

"I'm thinking about investigating any connection between Reed Harker's house blowing up and that backhoe at the Clement's building," Sharyn told them both when they were sitting down.

"Why?" Cari asked in disbelief.

"Because I think something else is going on here."

"Don't pay her no mind, Deputy," Ernie drawled. "She's been out in the sun too long. She gets this way from time to time."

Cari wished she shared the easy rapport that existed between the sheriff and Ernie. "I don't understand, Sheriff. What's going on?"

Sharyn looked at the files on her desk and pushed them aside. "There's no obvious connection between the two except for the protests over tearing down the Clement's building and making a park."

Ernie snapped his fingers.

Cari was lost. "What is it?"

"The Clement's Building."

"How does that affect anything?" the young deputy asked them.

"Let me see if I get this." Ernie ticked off. "Everybody knows that Harker has been leading the fight to tear down the building. He's been against the park idea from the beginning."

"And the explosion the other night is going to keep that from happening for a while," Sharyn finished.

Ernie shook his head. "That's all well and good. I agree that it fits together. In some weird way but it fits. What does it mean?"

"Someone thinks they can make it too hard to do anything but build a park?" Cari guessed.

"Right," Sharyn agreed with her.

"Except for a couple of things," Ernie told them. "First of all, the explosion at the building was an accident caused by wear. Second, Harker's house was an accident caused by faulty installation. The fire department signed off on both of them as accidents."

"The fire department is in ten different places at one time," Sharyn told him. "Did you see the look on their faces this morning? I'm not sure they're getting the right results."

"But Nick was there the other night at the backhoe fire. I saw his name next to Melinda Hays' on the report. He said the same thing."

"Maybe this person knows what the fire department looks for. He or she knows what to do to make it look like an accident."

Cari frowned. "Why would anyone go that far?"

"My aunt pointed out that a lot of the protesters lost family in the fire. There's some strong emotions backing the protests and maybe these two incidents. You probably don't recall, Cari, but the Clement's building fire was a big deal when it happened. Diamond Springs was shocked and outraged by it."

Ernie scratched his chin. "I suppose that makes sense."

"Humor me. Let's start looking at the protesters. Find out if any of them has a background for this type of thing. Find out which of them actually lost people in the fire. When we have that list, we can narrow it down to who had the opportunity."

"You know your Aunt Selma is in that group," Ernie reminded her. "Unless she was out of town, she had motive and opportunity. And I'll bet she has the knowledge to pull it off since she's been around farm equipment all of her life. And doesn't she have natural gas out there?"

Sharyn thought about it. "You're right. And you'll have to investigate her like any of the others. I don't believe

Selma feels that strongly about it. But she has a friend, Mary Ann Wagner, who lost a husband in the fire."

Cari shuddered. "I don't want to think anyone in this town did this! If the Harkers had been home—"

"But they weren't. Whoever did it probably knew that. Don't forget, they also waited until the construction crew was gone for the day to hit the backhoe. They might not want to hurt anyone. Just make their point. The problem is, someone could've been hurt. Maybe we can stop them before anything else happens."

Ernie nodded. "Okay. We'll get started on that list for you. Anything else?"

"Keep it low profile. I don't want to see this on the news tomorrow night."

Cari nodded solemnly. "You got it, Sheriff!"

Sharyn smiled as they left her office. Cari was a good choice for deputy. So was JP. She hoped Marvella would be too. She would be her last new deputy unless the county suddenly came into more tax money and wanted to share.

She wasn't complaining. They got two new cars, three new deputies, and a new phone system out of the last increase that the county made for them. They also had to pick up stray animals but it was worth the trade off. And there was always a chance that the new commission would change that again.

Ernie popped his head back in around the door. "Protests just got ugly down at the Clement's building. I was thinking about you coming and leaving Cari here."

"Let's do it!"

A crowd of about fifty or so people gathered at the burned out site. The remains of the backhoe were gone but in its place was another bright yellow backhoe and a truck to carry off debris. The protesters formed a ring around the equipment and were refusing to allow workers close to them. Sharyn glanced at the faces of the protesters, glad to see that Selma didn't make this one.

"Sheriff!" Jim Raymond hailed her. "One of my workers

was hit by a rock that one of those crazies threw at him. They need to be arrested."

She took off her hat and laid it in the backseat of the car. "I'll handle the protesters, Mr. Raymond. If the man who got hit with the rock wants to file a complaint, I'll arrest the rock thrower. But stay out of my way for now."

"I'll talk to him," he said quickly.

She approached the group of protesters. They were holding hands to form the circle that took in the equipment. "You all know this isn't going to help, don't you? And whoever threw that rock might be going to jail. The commission has made the decision about this area. This isn't the way to fight it."

"How can we fight then, Sheriff? We were excluded from that decision."

"Martha, you fight it with lawyers and through the government. You can't fight it in the street."

"It's too late for that!" another man shouted.

"You might be right," Sharyn agreed. "But this won't change what's going to happen here, Dan. This isn't the place to make your stand."

"You can't make us leave without arresting all of us," Mary Ann Wagner told her, grasping her friends' hands even tighter.

"Fact is, ladies and gentlemen." Ernie stepped forward. "We could arrest you all right now for trespassing. This is private property."

"You don't have enough room to hold all of us!"

"That may be true but we have the county jail and Stanley County would probably be willing to take some of you for a few days."

"You're bluffing," Harold Swinson yelled out. He was a local gunshop owner who helped them identify guns and markings on a few cases. "Nobody's gonna do anything this close to an election because it'll look bad to lock us all up. We have a legitimate grievance! We demand to be heard!"

His statement was followed by applause and shouts of

encouragement from the crowd that was growing on the street.

"This could get real ugly, Sheriff," Ernie whispered, drawing close to her. "How do you want to play it?"

Sharyn sighed. "As much as I hate it, this is the core of the protesters. One or more of them might be the people responsible for Harker's fire and the backhoe being destroyed. If they won't leave peacefully, we'll have to lock them up."

"You know what that would mean?"

"I know. Let me try one more time. Get on the radio and alert the county lock up."

Ernie went back to the car. The protesters all sat down on the ground and linked arms to prevent themselves from being taken away from the site.

"I don't want to have to do this, Martha, Harold, Ms. Wagner. I know all of you. I know you're good people. I know you don't want an arrest on your records. I know this is important to you or you wouldn't be here. If you leave now, we can forget the whole thing. Maybe you can get another hearing with the commission before they actually build on the site."

"They sold the land already," Martha told her. "They're going to put a parking deck here, Sheriff. Can you believe it? A pay-to-park lot! Where my brother died!"

Sharyn wished she could pick each of them up, take them home, and it would be over. She could empathize with them but she had to hold the line. "If you don't leave now, peacefully, I'm going to have to arrest all of you. I'm sorry. Please leave the area."

The group looked at each other then looked back at her. They didn't move. Their arms stayed linked. Their faces were set. They were staying the course.

Sharyn turned back to Ernie.

"They have some people on the way. We can hold half of them here. County can take the other half," he told her with the phone in his hand.

"All right." She took a deep breath. "We don't have any choice."

A step van from county picked up half of the protesters. The prisoners were quiet and subdued. They lay very still and made the deputies lift them into the vehicles. The crowd in the street was sympathetic and restless. Sharyn kept them back. She was worried about them getting involved and making the incident bigger than it already was. These people were friends and neighbors, not criminals. They were fighting for what they believed in. County commissioners were already calling for interviews to express their opinions on the subject. But the sheriff's office was the first in the line of fire.

The crowd booed when the last prisoner was taken away in the back of a sheriff's car. The construction crew moved in to resume work.

"Let's go home now," Sharyn told the people who remained. "There's nothing more to see."

People gave her dirty looks but they did as she requested and cleared the street. The crew foreman started his men working again. But an uneasy silence fell over the area.

Reporters were too late with camera crews but they followed the caravan to the sheriff's office. They used the building as a backdrop for their reports as they told the rest of the county what happened at the old Clement's building.

"What do we do now?" Cari asked when all of their prisoners were in holding cells.

Sharyn shrugged. "We process them. Don't send any of the paperwork to the DA's office yet. Maybe we can put a little fear into their hearts if we keep them for a while. We might not need to press formal charges against any of them."

Cari smiled. "Right, Sheriff."

At five P.M., Sheriff Sharyn Howard walked into the old courthouse for the debate. She was wearing her dress uniform. Roy Tarnower laughed as she was booed when she walked up the aisle to her place on the platform. She kept her back straight and her head high. All she could do was get through it.

Chapter Ten

"Look at her." Ernie pointed to the TV screen in the sheriff's office after tossing some popcorn into his mouth. "Cuts and bruises all over her face and they still booed her. What kind of town is this?"

Ed gave Trudy a quick wink then munched some popcorn too. "You know people are fickle, Ernie. They loved her yesterday but today she arrested a lot of their friends."

"Because they were doing something illegal!"

"I don't think they care," Nick said, taking some popcorn.

"It wasn't fair that only the people who belong to that club could go," Cari added. "We should've been there for her."

"She knows we're watching," Ernie told her. "She doesn't expect us to be there to hold her hand."

"It's too bad this happened just before the election." Trudy frowned at Ed after she blushed and spilled her Coke on her desk when he winked at her. "If they would've waited another week to get arrested, it would be over. She'll never win like this."

"Don't say that!" Ernie complained. "I don't want to retire yet."

Nick laughed out loud. "She's making Tarnower sound like an idiot. All he can do is repeat his stupid slogan about people going back to the good old days."

"Only now it's the good old days when friends didn't arrest friends," Ed mentioned. "He's versatile. You gotta give him that. The sheriff sounds good but Trudy's right. Unless she can chase down another bad guy in the next few days, I don't know if she can win this one."

"Excuse me?" Toby Fisher walked into the office to find them all hunched around the television screen. He smiled at Cari. "Mr. Percy sent me down to pick up those papers on the Chavis Whitley case."

Ernie shook his head. "Sheriff didn't sign off on that case yet."

They all looked at him.

Ed cleared his throat. "She's not having one of those *feelings* of hers about Chavis, is she?"

Ernie glared at him but didn't answer.

"Nick?" Ed tried to get the medical examiner's attention. "She's not, is she? You'd know because she'd ask you to do something stupid like look at all the bodies again."

Nick kept his eyes glued to the TV screen and didn't answer.

Ed raked his hands through his hair. "Oh, *man!*"

Cari ignored the conversation and smiled back at Toby. "This is almost over. The sheriff should be here in a few minutes. I think we're going to take her out for supper to cheer her up. You could stay and talk to her."

"Okay." He moved close to the desk where she was sitting. "Thanks. Do you have any idea when she plans to send the arrest papers to the DA's office for the protesters? Mr. Percy is anxious about processing that many people."

"I don't think she means to do that at all," Ernie answered.

Toby cleared his throat. "I don't think she can hold them like that, Deputy. Until the arrest is finalized and filed—"

"I don't think she means to finalize and file those arrests, son. Just take a seat and she can tell you herself when she gets back."

"Just planning on scaring them a little, huh?" Ed whispered to Ernie.

"You got it."

"And she wanted their names for the investigation," Cari said out loud, thinking to herself how cute Toby was when he smiled.

"What?" the assistant DA asked in surprise. "What investigation? She hasn't said anything to us about it."

Ernie's face was as cold as the face of Diamond Mountain after an ice storm. "Deputy Long? Do you have some paperwork to do?"

Cari blushed and stammered, "Uh, yes. Uh, sorry, Ernie."

"What's that all about?" Nick watched Toby follow Cari to the break room. He looked like a big puppy with an expensive briefcase.

"Sheriff's looking into the Harker house fire being related to the backhoe fire at the Clement's building. She thinks one of the protesters might be involved. She didn't want it spread around until she had something."

"I helped examine that backhoe," Nick replied. "It was an accident. My name is on the report."

Ernie shrugged. "Don't get all riled up. Ask her when she gets back. I just do what I'm told."

The debate was pre-recorded. The last of it was still on TV when Sharyn walked into the office. She wasn't surprised to see everyone watching it.

She left the old courthouse before anyone could ask her any questions about the debate or arresting the protesters. She was so tired she didn't know how much longer she could hold up her head. Her eyes felt gritty and her legs hurt.

The crowd at the debate was mean spirited. If she was scored on points she made off of Roy, she was pretty sure she was the winner. But she knew they were all judging her by the standard of what happened that day at the Clement's building. There wasn't anything she could do about that.

"Sheriff!" Trudy was purposely avoiding looking at Ed so she saw her first. "You were impressive!"

"Yeah, especially when you could hear me through the booing, huh?"

"You made Roy look like an old codger," Nick commented briefly. "Other people will see that, too."

"Thanks."

"Sheriff Howard." Toby approached her. "I was wondering about the Chavis papers? Mr. Percy would like to close up that case."

"I haven't had a chance to finish them," she lied. "Tell Mr. Percy I'll try to get to them when I'm not arresting protesters or chasing fires."

"Uh, sure. And what about this investigation into the fires?"

Trudy turned off the TV and the room got quiet. Cari folded her arms across her chest and looked at the floor.

Sharyn took a deep breath and released it. Her wool dress uniform was itchy around the neck and the hat was too tight on her head. It wasn't hard to guess that Cari told Fisher about the investigation. She needed to control the damage. "I think there might be a connection between the fires and the protesters. I'd appreciate it if you'd keep it to yourself until I have a chance to investigate. If it leaks out to the media, it would make things harder."

"Sure, Sheriff. I didn't know it was a secret." He glanced at Cari, surprised that she told him. "I won't tell anyone."

"Thank you. We'll keep the DA's office informed if there's any progress. Right now, we're just in the preliminary stages."

"All right. You'll send those Chavis papers to the office tomorrow then?"

"Yes."

"Thanks. And the charges against the protesters?"

"I don't plan to file any. I contacted the new owners of the land and they aren't interested in starting out here with a grudge against them. Besides the rock throwing incident, no harm was done. The construction worker who was hit by the rock declined to press charges against the woman who hit him. We're going to let them go later tonight."

Fisher frowned but didn't say anything. "All right, Sheriff. If you think that's best. It'll save a lot of paperwork." He smiled at Cari again. "Good night."

The office was silent after he left. He wasn't gone more than a minute when Cari jumped up and ran towards the door. "Oh, I forgot to give him . . . something. I'll be right back. Don't leave without me."

"We were going to take you out for supper at Fuigi's," Trudy told Sharyn quickly. "That's why we're all hanging around here like we don't have lives. How about it?"

"Sure. I need to change clothes then I'll be ready. Thanks." Sharyn looked around at her friends' faces. "Roy Tarnower might get this office but he'll never have a better group of people to work with."

"She looks dead on her feet," Trudy remarked when Sharyn went to the locker room and closed the door. "Bless her heart. She tries so hard."

"Jack Winter paid her another call last night," Ernie whispered. "With all this going on, he has to rear his ugly head."

Nick's look was murderous. "Too bad you didn't shoot him instead of Chavis."

"He's like a snake," Ed agreed. "What does he want with her anyway? The man's on her like a hound dog with a rabbit!"

Ernie's eyes were dark with apprehension. "I don't like to think what he wants with her. It makes me kind of queasy."

Cari returned and joined them. Her cheeks were pink and her eyes were sparkling. "Are you all talking about the sheriff and the old DA? Maybe they have a thing for each other."

Nick was sitting on one of the heavy wooden desks. He stood up so quickly that the telephone on the desk clattered to the floor. He picked it up and slammed it down before he muttered something like an apology then stormed off to the coffee machine.

"Bite your tongue!" Trudy chastened her. She glanced at

her watch. "What's keeping her anyway? I'm starving! I'm going to go and see if I can speed up the process!"

"Sounds like a good idea." Ed shot a sexy smile in her direction.

Trudy ran to the locker room to get away from him. She opened the door and peeked inside. "Sheriff? I haven't eaten since breakfast this morning and I'm—"

Sharyn was asleep in one of the chairs in the locker room. She made it into a gray sweatshirt and sweatpants. Her sneakers were sitting on the floor by her feet. Her head was tucked to the side, almost resting on her shoulder. She was breathing like an exhausted child.

Trudy covered her with her wool uniform jacket and turned out the light. She went back to the group and explained what happened. "I think she needs to sleep more than she needs to eat. But I'm still up for some burritos. Anybody else?"

Everyone else declined and started getting ready to go home.

Ed stepped closer to her. "I'm hungry too. I'll share some burritos with you."

Trudy thought better of it. "I think I'll just call it a night."

"What's wrong, Trudy?" Ed whispered. "Scared to go out with me?"

"Terrified."

Nick grabbed his coat and glanced towards the locker room door.

"She's fine," Ernie told him. "You worry too much."

"You're right." Nick thought better of it. "I'm going home. I'll see you tomorrow."

Ernie stared after him with a questioning gaze.

"Something wrong with Nick?" Trudy started putting on her jacket.

"Let me give you a hand with that," Ed offered, trying to hold it for her.

"No! Go away!"

Ed's downcast look was enough to make a stone cry. But Trudy was tougher and he left her alone.

"What's up with that?" Ernie laughed when he saw Ed leave.

"We were talking about Nick," she reminded him.

"I don't think anything's *wrong* with him, Trudy. He's just worried about the sheriff. It's . . . nice. So, what's up with you and Ed?"

"Nothing." Trudy sighed. "I'm going home."

Ernie called the county lock up and informed them that they could start releasing the protesters. Restin Lewis, the night sergeant, was glad to hear it. It looked like a mountain of paperwork to him and way too much trouble.

Ernie processed the protesters at the sheriff's office with JP's help while David went out on patrol. The protesters were even more subdued after spending some time in jail. Even the hardiest rabble-rouser simmered down. They were calmer than when they picked them up that day. Some of the women were a little weepy. The men were defiant but quiet about it. They called their friends and families to come and get them.

Ernie addressed them all while they were waiting to leave. "I want you to know that Sheriff Howard took a lot of flack from the media for what you people did wrong. But she was the one who made sure no charges were pressed against you so you could go home to your families. Don't let me see any of you here again. The next time we pick you up, it won't be this easy."

JP shook his head as the protesters went to meet their rides that were waiting outside the sheriff's office. "Think they learned anything?"

"I guess we'll see."

"The sheriff didn't do well tonight at the debate, huh?"

"Those things don't mean anything," Ernie explained. "Is this your first election here?"

J.P. grinned. "This is my first election *anywhere*! We had elections in Pátzcuaro. But most people didn't get to vote.

My family didn't own land. Everyone else made the laws for us."

"Well then you're in for a real treat. I feel more powerful with that ballot in my hand than I do with my gun. 'Course most of the time the people I elect shoot me in the foot. I could do it faster myself! But I voted in every election since I was twenty-one."

"I'm looking forward to it. I hope Sheriff Howard wins. My wife and I will vote for her."

"I hope so too."

"Me too." Sharyn wandered out of the locker room, still half asleep. "What time is it? What happened to dinner at Fuigi's?"

"It's almost midnight. Everyone else went home when you passed out back there. I knew you wanted these protesters out tonight so I stayed to help JP process them. David's out on patrol. Things are pretty quiet right now. How're you feeling?"

"Better." She yawned. "Now I feel like a truck rolled over me instead of a horse galloping across."

JP laughed. "You crack me out, Sheriff."

"Hungry?" Ernie asked her, ignoring JP's English snafu.

"Yeah. You know controversy always makes me hungry!"

"Come on. I'll buy you some waffles at the diner. Annie's spending the night with a girlfriend. I'm a free man for a few precious hours."

"Better not let Cari hear you say that," she told him after she pulled on her jacket and they walked outside. "She might take it the wrong way."

"Cari?"

"I think she has a little crush on you."

"Then you didn't see the way she was looking at assistant DA Fisher tonight. I could've smacked her when she told him about the investigation. It was all that smiling and eyelash batting. She wasn't thinking."

"Is that what happened?" Sharyn walked beside him on

the sidewalk. "Great! I don't suppose you'd like to pretend to be infatuated with her to keep her from telling Fisher everything we do before we do it?"

Ernie laughed. "Sure. Right after I crawl out of the cold grave that Annie puts me in when she hears the plan!"

They crossed the empty street and walked towards the neon diner sign. A growing orange light was dancing up from the ground in the distance, silhouetted against the black hulk of the mountain. Clouds hung low in the dark sky. Fog mingled with smoke on the cool autumn air.

"What's that?" Ernie pointed towards it.

Sharyn took out her cell phone. "How long ago did you release the protesters?"

He shook his head. "Just long enough, I guess!"

Chief Wallace stood back from the fires that his fire fighters were trying to put out. "This was a stupid, deliberate act of arson. Someone took a gas can and dumped half of it into the cab of the truck then poured the rest of it on the backhoe and lit it up! Might be kids."

"Half of the protesters weren't even released yet. County lockup was still processing," Ernie told Sharyn after talking to Restin Lewis on the phone. "That only leaves our group from our office."

"Get them all back in now!" Sharyn demanded. "If one of them is responsible, I want to know. This has got to stop!"

Ernie got back on the phone.

"I don't know what's got into these people," the chief said when Sharyn told him about the protesters. "But I think you should make whoever's responsible work the next few hours up on Diamond Mountain. Maybe that would help their attitude towards fire. My people are exhausted and overworked. Half of them are working with smoke inhalation."

"Maybe that would help," she agreed. "I'm sorry, Chief. I thought holding them for a while would make them think about it. I guess I was wrong."

"You did the best you could, Sheriff. Nobody wants to see people go to jail for what they believe. I think the commission should be taking the heat for this instead of you!"

"They probably would be if they were here arresting the protesters."

He laughed. "I know what you mean. It's hard being the person out front. But when they're giving me a hard time, it covers my people from getting harassed. I guess you do the same for your people."

"Where's Melinda tonight? I'm used to seeing the two of you together."

The chief blushed as deep red as his truck. "I hope it's not that obvious. She's taking some well deserved time off. I was a little jealous of the professor. She really looks up to him."

"She was a big help with that car fire. And if it makes you feel any better, I haven't heard any gossip about the two of you yet."

"That's good. My divorce isn't settled. Melinda's been like a storm in my life. I never saw it coming. She's a hard worker. She's been up on the mountain almost every day since the fire started. We've got some good people in this county. I can't tell you how many volunteers have stayed up there until I finally had to make them go home. Professor Thomopolis is another one. It must be great to know you can count on him with your work, too, huh, Sheriff?"

"Yeah. He's a good worker." She changed the subject as much for her own peace of mind as to ask Chief Wallace a few questions. "Any chance that the fires are related? Not just this one but the other backhoe fire and the Harker incident?"

"Anything is possible. But I looked over the Harker fire. The line separated between the stove and the wall. When you let natural gas escape and a spark happens, there's an explosion and fire. It's as natural as grits and butter. I've lodged a complaint with the state building inspectors about those houses."

"So you don't see any coincidence that this is all happening around the Clement's building protests?"

"I don't think so, Sheriff. Nick and Melinda did the work on the backhoe. They both thought it was wear and tear. Nobody wants to invest money back into equipment if they can help it. If you're talking about a serial arsonist, they all work the same. Not scattered like this. They have a routine they follow. I don't see any sign of that."

"Maybe not a serial arsonist," Sharyn stated, "so much as a person desperate to make a statement. They might know a little about covering it up. They aren't experts. Just lucky so far."

"I suppose it could happen. It wouldn't take much to separate the stove from the wall. They'd have enough time to get out before it blew. Someone could've made the gas line look like it was worn instead of cut. It could be hard to tell the difference after an explosion. This could go along with those other two. Someone fed up with the situation could've stopped by and tossed the gas."

"Will we be able to tell anything from the gas container?"

"I doubt it. It was left on top of the backhoe. Probably torched first. It's a slab of melted plastic. I might be able to find out what kind it was. That's about it."

"Thanks." She offered him her hand. "Whatever you can do."

"Sure thing, Sheriff. Say, how about locking up those protesters until the fires are out on the mountain? I don't need the extra overtime! The county is already complaining about too many hours."

"I'll do the best I can, Chief."

"We had twelve of the protesters at the office," Ernie told her when she finished with the chief. "Out of those, I can't reach three of them. The other nine are on their way in."

"Who are the three we can't reach?"

"Selma's friend, Mary Ann Wagner. The barber who

used to cut my daddy's hair, Max Thomas. And Tad Willis. You remember him."

"From the art gallery." She nodded. "Imagine him having a conscience about loyalty! Send David and JP out after them. I want to know where they are and where they've been since you released them."

They walked back to the office. Ernie spent the time on the phone. Sharyn shivered in her light jacket and thought again about getting her own place. There were several groups of apartments close by the sheriff's office. Not to mention Nick's building. It was too far to walk from there but it was a nice older building.

She crossed that off her mental list of possibilities. Diamond Springs was a small town and people loved to talk. She didn't want to see herself in Debbie Siler's gossip column.

Already a worried looking group of protesters was beginning to gather inside the sheriff's office. Angry spouses were demanding to know what was going on. Sleepy-eyed children yawned and curled up in chairs by the door.

"If there's anyone who'd like to tell us what happened out there tonight, we can work with you on a deal," Sharyn promised the nine protesters and their families who were there. Sharyn thought it might be better to take them in small numbers so they didn't have so much support from the other protesters.

"What are you taking about, Sheriff?" Martha asked bravely.

"I'm talking about another fire at the Clement's building. Someone spread gas on the truck and the backhoe that were left there tonight."

Martha shook her head. "I don't know who did it but I'm grateful to them."

"You might not feel too grateful if one of the fire fighters are hurt out there." She tried to get them to understand. "These men and women are fighting fires in the mountains and trying to keep up with what's going on down here. If you know something, you have to speak up!"

The group glanced at each other. No one said anything.

"All right. We're all going to the medical examiner's office. You'll have to remove your clothes and allow yourself to be checked for gasoline residue.

"David and JP have the other three with them," Ernie interrupted her.

"Have David bring them to the hospital."

"Are we under arrest?" Martha asked calmly.

"No, not yet," Sharyn replied.

"I think we should call our lawyers," she told the group. "I don't know if this is legal."

Sharyn folded her arms across her chest and sat back against Trudy's big desk. "Anyone who wants a lawyer present can call their lawyer. Anyone who feels the need to be arrested to have these tests done should tell me and I can accommodate them. We have to get to the bottom of these fires. One way or another."

None of them thought they should be arrested. Five of them agreed to the tests. Four of them called their lawyers. Ernie waited with them while Sharyn took the others to the hospital to be tested.

The morgue was impressively dark and cold. Probably another experience most of them never thought they'd have. Sharyn saw them looking around with fear etched keenly on their faces. Good. Maybe it would inspire one of them to speak up.

Nick was impassive as he directed them to cubicles where they could take off their clothes and put on hospital gowns. He tested their clothes and skin. There was no evidence of any gasoline on them. Sharyn talked to them afterwards. None of them had any idea about who started the fires. She told them to get dressed and go home.

Nick yawned. "That was a waste of time and sleep."

"Thanks for coming in. Ernie's on his way over with another group who have their lawyers with them. David and JP are still coming in with the last three."

He rubbed his face and eyes. "I might be too tired to tell if they have gasoline on them or not."

"I know what you mean." She slumped down in a chair beside him.

"Why didn't you tell me about Jack Winter sneaking into your house? That's one of those things we talked about in a relationship, remember? You tell me when things happen to you. I tell you when things happen to me. If Winter sneaked into my apartment, I'd tell you right away. It's called not keeping secrets from each other and making the other person find out from friends and co-workers."

She laughed. "I thought you said you didn't have much experience at relationships?"

"I'm serious, Sharyn. Why didn't you tell me?"

"I didn't see the point. I handled it."

"But you told Ernie."

"I work with Ernie."

"You work with me, too."

"And he doesn't get upset when things happen to me."

"Oh, no. He just shoots people!"

"Nick, Ernie and I have known each other a long time. I tell him things I don't tell everyone."

"Like that you didn't trust my findings on the backhoe fire and were investigating further?"

"Ernie and I have an important relationship."

"We have a relationship, too, Sharyn. Even if I didn't work with you, I'd tell you if Jack sneaked into my place."

She sighed. "Okay. I get the point. I'm sorry I didn't tell you. I'm not used to telling you things yet. I'll work on it."

"Thanks. I appreciate every consideration. What was Winter doing at your house?"

"I don't know. I think he's still looking for something my father left there. My mother trusts him completely. He didn't break in. He used her key."

"And how did you handle it?"

She looked down at her hands. "I broke into his house and threatened him."

"You did *what?*"

"Nick, you can't have it both ways. Either you want to know these things or you don't."

"Yeah. I'm so sure Ernie patted you on the head and told you that was the right thing to do."

She looked at him steadily. "I didn't tell Ernie. I knew how he'd react."

He smiled, pleased and surprised. "You mean you're telling me a secret Ernie doesn't know?"

"Yes. And I'd appreciate it if you keep it that way. Sometimes I feel like I live in a sound booth and the whole world is listening to the details of my life."

He touched her face gently. "Thank you."

"Don't start falling apart about it."

He cleared his throat and glared at her like a student who didn't do her homework. "Is that better? All right. I want to know everything. Why did you do it? He could've had you arrested. Or worse."

"You've been talking to Ernie."

"Yeah. *He* talks to me!"

"He thinks Winter has a crush on me or something, right?"

"Does he?" Nick was direct. "Does Jack Winter have a thing for you?"

"I don't know." She stood up again. "It's complicated. I told you that he asked me out."

"But that was when he was still the DA. I thought he just wanted to control you."

"And that's so much better?"

They were interrupted by Ernie and his four protesters. They brought noisy lawyers with them who wanted to be part of the process for their client's sake. One of the younger women kicked her lawyer out when the man insisted on being there when she changed clothes.

Before they could finish with that group, David and JP brought in the rest. Tad Willis was spouting out about being American and having his rights violated. Mary Ann Wagner was quiet but angry. She promised Sharyn that her aunt would hear about the indignity she put her through. Max Thomas was cooperative, more afraid than the rest. He told Sharyn right away that he wasn't responsible for what happened.

"Do you have any idea who *is* responsible for it?" she asked him quietly, leading him away from the group.

He nodded towards Mary Ann. "Her. I think she's crazy. She keeps talking about the dead sleeping in the building."

Sharyn looked up at him from her notebook. "Why are you involved, Mr. Thomas?"

"Me? I was bored. Not much to do since I closed down the barbershop. Not anymore. I didn't know I was going to get arrested and strip searched!"

None of the twelve protesters tested positive for gasoline residue on their skin or clothes.

"Maybe they washed it off," David said helpfully.

"They couldn't completely," Nick informed him. "Even if they changed clothes, some of it would've stayed with them. These people were clean."

"You'll be hearing from me, Sheriff Howard," one of the lawyers told her on his way out. "And good luck with your re-election campaign."

"Lawyers creep me out." David shuddered.

"I'm a bar exam away from being one," Sharyn told him. "At least they don't have to be re-elected."

"Good point," Ernie agreed with her. "Now what?"

"We go back to square one. Unfortunately, we've lost the element of surprise. This will be in the paper by morning."

"Maybe even on CNN," JP added with a grin.

"That's not a good thing, JP," Ernie pointed out.

"Oh. Sorry. My wife loves to see me on TV."

Sharyn stood up. "I'm going home and leaving you boys to it. Ernie, I'll let you take me home. Tomorrow, we'll pull all the records from the old Clement's fire investigation and sort out the protesters who lost someone from the ones who didn't. They're probably our best bet for the fires."

"But none of them had gasoline on them," JP reminded her.

"I know. But our arsonist is out there somewhere. It's as good a place as any to start. Maybe now we have their attention."

Chapter Eleven

It was Monday morning, the day before the election. The smoke was so thick around Diamond Springs that people used their windshield wipers and turned on their headlights even after sunrise. The Gazette carried a large piece about the sheriff's office arresting the protesters. It included the fact that they were looking for an arsonist. The investigation into the protesters' lives and backgrounds was criticized. There was a small piece about the debate. The paper called it a draw. They were still endorsing Roy Tarnower.

Sharyn's mother woke her at five A.M. to watch a story on CNN about the embattled sheriff of Montgomery County, North Carolina. It carried scenes from her first election then switched to the protesters being arrested. They highlighted her two-year career fairly, citing how low she was in the polls to win the election.

"It doesn't look good for you," her mother said. "I'll make you some pancakes."

"I don't think I can eat. Thanks anyway." Sharyn climbed out of bed, grateful that she was able to get some sleep. She didn't think she'd ever be able to sleep in the house again. But she was too exhausted to care when she got home last night.

When she was showered and dressed in her uniform, she went to the kitchen and poured herself a cup of coffee. She knew she'd miss the memories that were trapped in the house, frozen in time. She could almost hear Kristie's laughter as she badgered her for a ride to school. Her father giving his uniforms to her mother to take to the dry cleaner. That feeling of being part of a family that died the day her father was killed.

"Mom." Sharyn decided to broach the subject. "After the election, I'm going to look for my own place. Closer to the office."

Faye stopped ironing and stared at her. "I know we have our differences but you don't have to move out."

"It doesn't have anything to do with that. I think we get along okay. But I can't live here with you forever. I might be the oldest person still living at home with her mother."

"Is this about you and Nick?"

"No. I'm not moving in with him or anything like that. I need my own place."

"Sharyn, this *is* your own place. This is your home. It will look bad if you move out on your own before you're married."

"I don't plan on getting married for a long time." Sharyn laughed at the thought. "But I can't live here anymore."

"It's Jack, isn't it?" Faye nodded and resumed her ironing. "He told me you two had a confrontation the other night when I sent him here for my sweater."

"He wasn't here for your sweater. He was in Dad's den and he shut me in my closet. He sneaked in to try to find whatever he thinks Dad kept here that could hurt him. He might already have it now. He was pretty calm about it."

"You've been so hard since your father died. You don't trust anyone. You see some kind of plot in everything. Jack has been a good friend. He was a good friend to your father. I might even consider marrying him."

"Has he proposed to you?" The idea made Sharyn gag. As much as she disliked Caison Talbot, this was much worse.

"No. But we're very close."

Sharyn drew a deep breath. She didn't want to say anymore. "I have to go to work, Mom. Please don't trust Jack.

He's headed for a bigger fall than Caison. Separate yourself from him before you get hurt again."

"Thank you for your concern." Faye blinked tears from her eyes. "You better go along now so you're not late."

It was awkward but Sharyn hugged her. They looked at each other across the old ironing board. The flower-covered board was like the years of misunderstanding and hard feelings that stood between them.

"Go on now," Faye urged her, patting her hair to be sure it was still in place. "You have a town to protect. Be careful, Sharyn."

"I will, Mom."

Joe was waiting in the drive to take her to the office. "Sorry I didn't come in. I wasn't sure what the right protocol was for picking up the sheriff."

"That's okay. Thanks for the ride." Her cell phone rang as she closed the door to the cruiser. "Sheriff Howard."

It was Nick. "I hope you slept well."

"I did, thanks."

"I finished with Chavis and maybe with the whole talcum powder theory."

"Okay. What's up?"

"There was no talcum powder on Chavis' body. I sent the kids out to check his house. Nothing there either. We checked his Durango again. Zip. With everything that's been going on, the fire department isn't sure who responded to the car fire. I checked with the paramedics who picked up Goodson's body. None of them use talcum powder when they put on their gloves."

She sighed. "I guess that's a dead end then."

"Really dead. One of the people here quit yesterday to go home to California. He was responsible for transporting bodies to the morgue after they got to the hospital. He could be the source. I don't know. If he was, I don't think he was involved in both deaths. He's a nineteen-year-old kid who was going to school here. I have his name, address and phone number if you want it."

"Keep it on file. Thanks for checking it out, Nick."

"Sure. I'm sorry, Sharyn. If there's anything else that links Goodson and Monte besides Chavis, I don't know what it is."

"Yeah, me either. I'll talk to you later."

"How about dinner?"

"Maybe."

"I'll call you after my classes."

"Okay." Sharyn closed her cell phone.

Joe backed the car down the driveway. "Bad news?"

"Worse. No news."

Ernie was waiting for them when Sharyn got to the office. She was surprised and pleased to see her Jeep already parked in the back lot. The paint was shiny and red. No marks on it. The new windshield was blemish free.

"They threw in a free paint job," Ernie said, handing her a bunch of papers to sign.

"They did a good job. I hope it runs okay."

"You mean that you have brakes again?" His mustache twitched. "That was quite a stunt you pulled. I'm surprised you didn't flip it over."

She signed the papers and handed them back to him then took her coffee from him. "So was I."

"I've got Cari going full speed ahead on the arson investigation. I'm walking over to the old courthouse myself for the records of the fire. They're too old to be in the system. I'll have to make copies of them."

"I'll walk over with you unless there's something else pressing?"

"Reed Harker is waiting for you in your office. He wants to know what progress we've made towards solving his arson case now that the Gazette told him that he *has* an arson case. Eldeon Percy wants a word with you about the Chavis case. He's waiting for a call. You got some roses from Jack Winter that I sent to the hospital to beautify their lobby. And Chief Wallace wants a word with you about making the fire department sound incompetent by investigating the arson cases without them."

She shuddered. Her nose itched like she was going to

sneeze from thinking about the roses. "I'll walk over there with you."

He laughed. "I thought so. Feeling a little embattled this morning, huh?"

"You saw it?"

"Yeah. Annie recorded it for you in case you missed it."

"That was nice of her."

"She thought you looked real good on the screen."

Sharyn quietly said good morning to Trudy then had her hold her calls until she got back from the courthouse. She managed to sneak out of the office before Commissioner Harker saw her.

"You'll have to talk to him sometime," Ernie told her.

"I know. If he's still here when I get back, I'll talk to him."

They crossed the street together. The old courthouse had been sitting in that same spot for almost two hundred years. For its anniversary, it was restored and converted into a storage facility and a civic center for small events like the debate. The golden spire was almost hidden by the heavy smoke from the mountains.

"Did the chief say anything about the fire situation up there?" Sharyn asked him.

"Yeah. He said it was about the same. They're holding their ground but the fires are still burning."

"We need rain." She used her key to open the door to the courthouse. She sniffed. "That smoke gets into everything."

Ernie pointed to the stairs that led to the record storage. "I don't think so. Look!"

A small stream of white smoke was wafting down from upstairs. Ernie took out his cell phone to call 911. "Sharyn!" he yelled as she ran up the stairs, "get back from there!"

She didn't listen. A fire in the records area would mean losing a hundred years of police and local records. The building itself was irreplaceable. She followed the smoke into the record storage area. The fire was contained to a trashcan. She knocked over the can and stamped out the fire as the sound of sirens came down the street outside.

Ernie coughed as he caught up with her. "That was a stupid thing to do."

"They're documents from storage." She sifted through the black ash. That was all she could tell about them. They were burned too badly to read.

He pressed his white handkerchief to his nose and mouth. "How much you wanna bet that those are the records of the Clement's fire?"

"Pretty brazen. Wouldn't that show us we're on the right track?"

"Maybe. Or whoever started it thought the building would burn before anybody noticed."

The fire fighters raced into the courthouse and ushered Ernie and Sharyn out the front door.

"There's too many keys to this place," Ernie said, looking around outside. "There's also an open window on the ground floor. They didn't even need a key."

Sharyn saw a faint white dusting on the damp window ledge. She pulled Ernie back. "Hold on a minute. Let's get a sample of this."

He held out his handkerchief while she used her credit card to scrape some of the powder off the ledge. "What do you think it is?"

"Talcum powder?"

"You think this is the same stuff?"

"I don't know. Let's see if we can get any prints from the ledge."

There was a clear handprint on the bright green ledge. The morning dew combined with the powder and sealed it. Ernie found another on the file cabinet where the records were stored. "Whoever did this took the records from the fire. Probably saw in the paper this morning that we were looking into it."

"That's it?" she asked him, still looking over the scene. Fireman's boots had muddied the carpets and wood floors in the building. They used a fire extinguisher to make sure the fire was out. White foam was spread out on top of the black paper ash in the trashcan and the floor around it.

"I can't tell without reading the records of everything in here. But the files for the fire are gone."

"I'm going to seal this off for now and call Nick to come and compare his glove prints with these."

Ernie was amazed. "You know what that would mean?"

"The fires and the two deaths are related?"

"All of it might be linked to the Clement's building fire. Maybe Chavis was a scapegoat."

"There was no way to know that," she rushed to assure him. "We did the best we could."

"I don't feel bad about his loss, Sheriff. He was scum."

She knew him better than that but she didn't push the issue. She looked at the ashes and the white foam. "Without those documents we're at a standstill."

"Somebody else must have those files."

Sharyn snapped her fingers. "Capitol Insurance. They won't know much about the investigation done here but they've been doing their own investigation for the past ten years. Maybe it will be enough material to give us what we need."

Ed and Joe were on patrol handling a report of car theft and burglary. Ernie got in touch with the insurance company. They agreed to have the documents from their records and investigation sent to us. They will be here by the afternoon.

Cari sat in front of the sheriff's big desk with Ernie. "I just want you to know how grateful I am for another chance, Sheriff."

"You're welcome, Cari," Sharyn told her. "But if anything like that happens again, I'll let you go."

"Yes, ma'am."

"So the records are being shipped over," Ernie informed them both. "In the meantime, we gotta think about the big picture here. If this fire and the handprints on the window ledge at the courthouse link these events together, why would our arsonist kill Goodson and Monte Blackburn?"

"Well, Goodson is obvious," Cari conjectured. "He didn't push hard enough for the memorial park. The protesters could blame him for that."

"That's true," Sharyn agreed. "And Monte lived under the building. Maybe he saw something he wasn't supposed to see."

Ernie took out his notebook. "Maybe whoever is responsible for all of this was there first, looking the place over."

"Getting ready for the main event?"

"Yeah."

Sharyn stood up. "Come on. We're going to have to drag Nick out of that classroom."

"I can't leave yet," Nick told Sharyn plainly. "I'm giving exams. They pay me to do this."

"I need to see those talcum glove prints." She kept her voice down outside the classroom door. "I think we might have a match for them at the old courthouse."

He shook his head and glanced back at the room full of psychology students. "I can't leave them here alone."

Sharyn put her hand on Cari's shoulder. "Deputy Long. I have a new assignment for you."

"Sheriff? I can't teach a class!"

"You don't have to teach," Nick explained. "When it's ten, they're finished. Make sure they don't get up and wander around. Collect the papers and wish them well."

Cari swallowed hard. "Okay."

Sharyn nodded to Nick. "Let's go."

Nick lifted prints from the window frame, the file cabinet and the trashcan. All three were covered in talcum powder. All three matched each other and the fragments he found on Goodson and Monte. He saved each of them separately then took off his black rimmed glasses. "I guess this links the break-in at the courthouse and that fire with Monte and Goodson's death."

"I think so. There may be a link to the other fires. They already hauled away the backhoe and started work on Harker's house. It might be hard to get anything there."

"But you'd like me to try?"

"Yes." She smiled. "Thanks."

"Anything for the embattled sheriff of Montgomery County. Too bad they aren't real prints and we could find out who did it. Maybe that would give you a better chance in the election."

"Is everyone up at five A.M. watching TV?"

"What else?"

She looked at him steadily. "Do you really think I'll lose the election?"

"I think no one knows until the ballots are counted. You've done a good job for the city and the county. In the end, I think that will matter more than hype."

"Thanks. That's pretty positive coming from you!"

"I can be positive. Want to drive over to the Harker house with me?"

"I'd like to but I can't. I left a mess at the office and I have to go back and handle it. Maybe we can still have dinner? Call me."

Sharyn went back to the office and marched in to confront Reed Harker. He was still there waiting for her.

"Where are you in the investigation, Sheriff?"

"I'm getting started, Mr. Harker, and as soon as I know something new—"

"Not good enough! Someone blew up my house! I want to know who it was."

"And as soon as I know—"

"I want the full department on this." He got to his feet. "I expect a report from you by tonight!"

She stood up and put out her hand. "I'll do the best I can, sir."

"I'm staying at the Y. I left my wife and kids with her mother. If there's a chance it could happen again, I don't want them here. I never thought something I did on the commission could hurt them."

"You did what you thought was best." Sharyn felt sorry for him. "That's all any of us can do."

"Thanks, Sheriff. Please call me if you learn anything."

"I will, sir."

She barely had time to sit down before Eldeon Percy swept into her office. Trudy was following right behind telling him that Sharyn was busy. He didn't care. He closed the door in her face and turned to smile at Sharyn. "Your secretary is very efficient. She's kept me waiting on the line for over an hour."

"Sorry, sir. But I'm not ready to close on the Chavis case. There's new evidence that points to another person being involved in the murders."

"Another person?" Percy dusted off the chair with his white handkerchief then sat down. "Sheriff, your reputation for flights of fancy proceeds you."

Her jaw clenched. "This isn't a flight of fancy, sir. We have proof." She told him about the glove prints and the talcum powder.

He nodded with his eyes half closed, listening. How many times she watched him in court as he adopted that pose. He looked like a sleeping tiger. She recalled thinking as a child that he was so old he couldn't stay awake. Her father laughed when she told him. He explained that when she saw Mr. Percy close his eyes, he was about to make something happen.

"I think you should proceed, Sheriff," he said finally, opening his eyes. "It sounds like maybe we blamed Mr. Chavis too quickly."

"The evidence did point to him, sir."

"I understand. Good detective work, young woman. Make sure you keep me informed before the press from now on, okay?"

"I'll do the best I can, sir."

He touched his icy fingers to hers before he left. Sharyn sat down hard on her chair, amazed and a little scared.

"Did Percy bust your chops about Chavis?" Ernie asked, coming in when he saw that the DA was gone.

"No. He agreed with me."

"Really?" He scratched his head. "Will wonders never cease?"

"I know. Maybe we're still in that horror movie and a pod has taken over him."

"Maybe." He laughed with her. "But I think you're getting your horror movies confused."

"Anything yet on that insurance investigation?"

"We got the papers about an hour ago. Now we have to wade through them."

"I wasn't able to reach Chief Wallace. Let me give you a hand."

They poured through the thousands of documents that made up the case file. There were reports from the fire. Autopsies on the dead. Eyewitness accounts of the living. Some of the documents were copies of the sheriff's department files. Some were from the fire department.

"No wonder they couldn't ever find who did it," Ernie remarked. "They must've talked to each person a hundred times and asked the same questions over and over."

"You remember it, don't you?" Sharyn asked him. "Did you have any suspects?"

Ernie played with his mustache. "As I recall, there were a few that your daddy and I narrowed it down to. There was a security guard who was fired the week before. There were a couple of disgruntled employees who didn't receive their raises or some such. All of them had alibis we couldn't break through. It was like sifting through a big pile of soap bubbles. We couldn't come up with anything we could hold on to."

"It doesn't look like this private investigating team did any better," Cari remarked.

"Well, we have to start somewhere." Sharyn picked up a sheet of names. "Let's find out how many of these people are still in Diamond Springs, alive, and able to get around. That will narrow the list."

Each of them took a sheet of thirty-six names.

"The ones underlined in red are the ones who died in the fire," Ernie explained. "We know we can't find them so maybe we should concentrate on people close to them."

They split up and went to their computers. Sharyn was

besieged by calls. Reporters wanted interviews before the election. Chavis Whitley's sister was upset because she wanted to claim her brother's body and give it a proper burial so she could have her lawyer check into his finances.

Nick called to tell her that he was able to find one partial print on the stove in Harker's house. "It's not much but after comparing all of them, I believe they're from the same person. I don't know how well that will hold up in court. We don't have fingerprints, just glove prints. Anybody could've been wearing those gloves even if we find who they belong to."

"I know," she agreed. "If we actually find a suspect, we should be able to match his DNA to the gloves, right?"

"Right. If you find a suspect. Tell Deputy Long that I'll pay her to come back and stare at my students," he remarked with a laugh. "Apparently most of them failed the test because they forgot to cheat."

"Was it the gun?"

"I don't think so. Most of the class is male."

"I'll tell her."

"Still on for dinner?"

"I don't know." She rubbed her hands across her eyes. "We're sorting through the insurance investigation. I can't believe how hard it is to find these people."

"Okay." He sighed. "I'm grading exams if you need me. If you're not done by six, I'm dragging you out somewhere anyway."

She laughed. "Big talk. Must be the new SUV!"

"See you later."

With a sigh, wishing she was doing anything else but going through names with a computer, Sharyn resumed her search. She was down to fifteen names when Ernie knocked on her door.

"Cari and I are going out for a bite. Want to come?" he asked her, cleaning his glasses with a napkin.

"Go ahead. I'm waiting for Nick at six. How are you two doing with your names?"

"Cari has six dead, twelve no longer living here. I have three dead, eighteen no longer living here."

"You're both ahead of me," she told him. "I have three dead, twelve no longer living here."

"You are a mite slow. Must not be spending enough time on your computer!"

She put down what she was working on. "Do you get the feeling this might be a dead end?"

He shrugged. "We won't know until we go through all of it. If it involves the Clement's building, the person has to be here."

The phone rang. "I hope that's Chief Wallace. I've been trying to get in touch with him all day."

Ernie waited while she answered the phone. Cari joined them.

"It was someone else looking for him," Sharyn said as she hung up the phone. "I've called his house and his cell phone all day with no answer. Now they say he hasn't checked in with any of the fire crews."

"What's up with that?" Ernie frowned as he considered it.

"I don't know." She glanced at her watch. "I guess I'll take a swing by his house and see if everything's okay. Then Nick should be here and I'll take a break too."

"Want me to come with you?"

"No. It should be fine. He's probably too exhausted to get up. But there's too much weird stuff going on to take any chances."

"What weird stuff?" Ed asked, peeking around the corner.

"Trying to locate Chief Wallace," Ernie explained. "The sheriff says he's been missing all day. I was offering to go with her because of the weird stuff going on. She was politely declining."

Ed nodded. "I know how she is. But I'm going off-duty. David traded me a few hours so he's coming in early. I have a special date tonight. Chief Wallace lives out my way. How 'bout I tag along and you drop me off at home?"

"Can't argue with that reasoning." Ernie looked at Sharyn.

"All right." She got up and picked up her hat. "Let's go."

The Jeep ran perfectly. The chief lived a few miles outside of town going towards Harmony. The twisting roads were mostly gravel going back to his house.

"You didn't ask me who my date is tonight," Ed reminded her when they finished talking about the murder cases.

"Okay. Who's your date tonight, Ed?"

"Trudy."

Sharyn almost ran off the road. "Trudy? I would've thought she knew better!"

"Sheriff!" He looked hurt. "What's wrong with me dating Trudy?"

"Nothing. I'm just surprised."

"If you're thinking this is like Cari or any of the other women, you're wrong. I'm not going out with Trudy because she's gorgeous or sexy and she sure isn't young."

"That speech is what must've sold her on the idea," she joked.

"I don't mean that she's *not* gorgeous and sexy. But she's my age. When have you ever known me to date a woman my age?"

"I don't know if I ever noticed, Ed. It was enough that you didn't want to date me!"

"I left that to David. But I guess it was always Nick, huh? Anyway, it wouldn't be me because I think of you as that little sassy kid who used to beg me for gumball money. That's a little too young. Even for me."

Sharyn pulled up into the chief's yard. The house was quiet in the late afternoon sun. "His truck is here. I told Ernie he was probably sleeping. The man has to be exhausted." She tried calling him again on her cell phone.

"Dennis Wallace is a good man. We used to go the beach together on our motorcycles when we were in school. My mama is his second cousin."

"No answer." She closed the phone again and looked at the house. It was a long, flat ranch style with white shutters and salmon-colored brick. Something didn't feel right.

Ed was doing the same. "You know, I don't like it. I don't know why. But there's something wrong."

"I was thinking the same thing. The door to the pickup is half open."

"And I can hear his dog barking inside. How could he sleep through that?"

"The outside porch light is on," Sharyn said. "His evening paper is still out there."

Ed got out of the Jeep with his gun in his hand. Sharyn did the same. They approached the pickup and glanced inside. The chief's hat and gloves were on the seat. The radio was paging him over and over.

"Engine's cold." Ed looked at the house again. The dog was still barking. "What do you think, Sheriff?"

"I think we should be careful. Maybe he's been putting out too many fires and they made him a target too."

Ed nodded. "I'll go in through the back."

"Where's his bedroom?"

"Back that way." He pointed. "Kitchen in back, living room in front. Three bedrooms at that end."

"All right."

The front door was open. The keys were in the lock. Sharyn crept into the house, sniffing the air. There was no sign of gas or smoke. There was also no sign of the chief. She prowled through the house, finally meeting Ed in the hallway coming back from the bedrooms.

"Nothing."

"I know. Where is he?"

"It doesn't look like he's been here since last night," Ed observed. "Looks like he parked the truck and started inside but left again real fast."

"Without his truck." Sharyn holstered her gun. "Something *is* wrong here, Ed."

They got back in the Jeep after Ed left food and water

for the chief's dog. Sharyn called the office to have Ernie put out an APB on Chief Wallace.

"Will do." Ernie wrote it down. "You think something's happened to him and he's not just up on the mountain?"

"I think he was here, Ernie, but it looks like he left really fast. His truck is here. His front door was open with his keys still in the lock. I don't like it."

"Okay. Nick is here. He says it's six and he's hungry."

"Put him to work on my list of names until I get back," Sharyn answered. "And let me know if you hear anything about the chief."

"Yes, ma'am."

"Dennis could be on the mountain with someone else," Ed said as they left the house. "Maybe he didn't realize he left his keys in the door."

"Maybe."

"What are you thinking? I know you're not even considering that this looks bad for him."

"I didn't say that, Ed." She turned down the road to go to his house. "You must be thinking the same thing."

"I wouldn't think that about him! I told you, I've known him my whole life. Dennis wouldn't kill anybody. He sure wouldn't start any fires."

"Most arsonists are fire fighters. Did you know that? Dennis is the fire chief now. He's been a fire fighter for years. He's under a lot of stress."

"I don't care. You're barking up the wrong tree, Sheriff."

Ed's house was only a few minutes away. He climbed out of the Jeep and looked back at her. "Dennis isn't a killer. Give me some time to find him, huh?"

"You might be better at it than the highway patrol. Do what you can. But be careful. If something's wrong with the Chief, Ed, he could hurt you."

"I will be." He sighed. "Trudy is never going to believe this."

She laughed. "Yes, she will!"

Sharyn left him there and headed back towards Diamond

Springs. Her phone rang again and she answered it, hoping it was the chief and everything was all right.

"Head back quick!" Ernie said without preliminary.

"What's wrong?"

"Your mama's house is on fire. Fire fighters say she's trapped inside!"

Chapter Twelve

Sharyn rarely used her siren and lights. She put them on now and sped down the roads towards her house. She thought about her words to her mother that morning and her insistence on moving out. Her mind raced faster than her Jeep to recall walking into the local convenience store and seeing her father's bleeding body on the floor. She put her foot down harder on the gas and tried to think like the sheriff instead of a frightened daughter.

Was this a legitimate fire or something caused by her looking into the case so closely? Like Chief Wallace, she supposed she could be a target. She knew they didn't question all the protesters. There were at least fifty at some of the other rallies she saw on TV. Just because the twelve they released didn't test positive for gasoline residue didn't mean someone else in the group wasn't responsible.

She saw the gray smoke for a few miles before she reached her house. Even with the smoke from the mountains, it was easy to tell them apart. She heard the fire engines being called to the scene and knew that Ernie and Cari were already there. Her thoughts flew ahead of her, praying she wouldn't get there to find her mother badly burned or dead. There was only so much time to get out. The hallway was so small coming from the bedrooms.

It felt like it took a year for her to crawl to the edge of the street. All of their neighbors were out, pointing and talking about the fire. Flames still raced through the front of the house and the roof. She parked the Jeep, left the door open, and ran to Ernie. "My Mom—"

"Over there with the paramedics." He took her arm. "She got a little smoke, that's all."

Sharyn felt like she was going to faint. She put her head down and tried to breathe. Relief washed over her but her heart was still racing.

Ernie sat her down on the backseat of the patrol car behind her. "Stay there for a few minutes. She's okay. You'll just be in the way over there. We're going to talk to a few people who claim they saw what happened. Breathe, Sharyn. She's gonna be fine."

Cari walked quickly up the Howard's front lawn beside Ernie. "Is she okay? I never saw the sheriff like that before."

"They called her to the convenience store after her daddy was shot two years ago. She watched that crazy man hurt her sister. I imagine the idea that her mama was hurt was enough to throw her into a tailspin."

"I wouldn't hold up that well," Cari admitted.

"Me either. Just thinking that Annie could've been hurt was enough for me. I shut down and couldn't even do my job."

"Guess that's why she's the sheriff."

"Guess so."

Sharyn was back up on her feet and breathing normally in a few minutes. Thankfully, there weren't any reporters there until after she recovered. She wasn't sure what would've happened to her if her mother was hurt or worse. She didn't want to think about it.

Faye smiled at her daughter and grabbed her hand. "It was terrible, Sharyn! I heard the window crash and then I smelled smoke. I looked out of the bedroom door and your father's den was on fire. I screamed and ran out of the house."

Sharyn hugged her close. "That was exactly the right thing to do."

"But what about your grandmother's china? And Aunt Sarah's chintz curtains? And your father's things." She sobbed daintily against Sharyn's shirt.

"None of those things matter as much as you getting out safely," Sharyn assured her. "I was so worried when I got the call. Are you sure you're all right?"

The paramedic nodded. "She's fine. She got out of there right smart."

Kristie and Selma pulled up in Selma's old station wagon. Kristie was already crying as she threw herself into her mother's arms.

Selma patted Sharyn's shoulder. "What happened here?"

"I don't know yet. I'm about to find out."

Ernie nodded to Mr. Daggot, the Howard's next-door neighbor, and walked towards her. "Cari's still asking around but Mr. Daggot says a man on a motorcycle tossed something on fire through the den window."

"Through the den window?" Sharyn glanced at the house she grew up in. The picture windows in the front room were at least ten feet wide and six feet high. There was only one window in the den. It was only three feet wide and four feet high, almost hidden behind some bushes. "That was a tough target."

"Your mama said the same thing. She ran out through the front door. She saw the den on fire but nothing else."

"Sharyn!" Nick left his SUV on the street and ran towards them. "Is Faye okay?" He looked at her closely. "Are *you* okay?"

"We're both fine," she answered, looking around the crowded yard. The election signs were trampled into the green grass and red clay.

He put his arms around her and held her tightly for a few moments, saying against her hair, "I would've been here sooner but I got a call from the lab in Raleigh that's been looking at those talcum powder samples."

She stepped away from him. "What did they find?"

"Traces of Halon."

She nodded. "Like the foam they sprayed in the courthouse?"

"No. The fire department had to stop using Halon in 1994. They decided it was bad for the ozone and banned it. Apparently, whoever moved those bodies and started the fire in the old courthouse has Halon residue on their gloves."

Ernie chewed over his words like an old dog with a sock. "Someone who worked with it before. Maybe still has access to it."

"All of the samples of talcum powder match," Nick continued. "We've got the glove prints. But it's still all circumstantial."

"Chief Wallace is missing," Sharyn told them. "That's not circumstantial."

"You don't think he's involved, do you?"

"I don't know. Ed is sure that he's not. He says they've been friends all of their lives." She shook her head. "He also said they used to ride motorcycles to the beach when they were kids."

"He'd have access to Halon," Nick said. "He could have residue on his gloves from using it before."

Ernie turned to Cari. "Call DMV and see if the chief has a motorcycle listed in his name."

"One step ahead of you," she said with the cell phone at her ear.

"We have to get in touch with Ed." Sharyn was worried about her deputy. "If this is true, the chief is dangerous and probably doesn't want to be found."

"No motorcycle listed to Dennis Wallace." Cari closed her cell phone.

"That doesn't prove anything," Ernie responded, pushing his hat back on his head. "He could've borrowed one or stolen one."

Sharyn looked at her house again. The fire fighters were finishing up. The right end of the house almost looked normal. The left end was in bad shape. The roof was blackened and had holes in places. All of the windows were broken out. She didn't want to think what her bedroom looked like. "Let's not try to put this together with the other acts. Not yet anyway. Let's concentrate on finding Chief Wallace. What about getting a search warrant for the chief's house and his locker at work? We could see if he has any gloves that fit the pattern."

"I'm on it." Ernie nodded. "Come on, young 'un."

Sharyn checked with her mother. She was going home with Selma and Kristie. A long, black Lincoln pulled up in the street. Senator Caison Talbot pushed himself slowly out of the car while his driver held the door for him. Selma, Kristie, and Sharyn watched as Faye ran down the hill and threw herself into his arms.

"There's hope for the old girl yet!" Selma slapped her thigh.

"I guess they really do love each other." Kristie smiled and linked her arm through her sister's.

"I guess so." Sharyn watched the couple together. "I have to go. The fire chief's missing and we think we might have a link to everything that's been happening."

"Not Mary Ann!" her aunt said hopefully.

"Not Mary Ann," Sharyn returned. "I was more worried about *you* being the main suspect!"

Selma laughed. "You come up with the funniest things! I'm gonna be picking figs next week. Whether you win this election or not, make sure you come by and get some."

Sharyn hugged her. "I will. See you later, Kristie."

Nick was still waiting for her by her Jeep. "Looks like you might be in line for a new daddy anyway."

"At least it's not Jack!"

"I can't believe you're willing to take Talbot over *any-body*!"

"Some devils are just worse than others."

"Don't I know it!" He kissed her forehead. "I guess I gave away the secret back there."

She hugged him. "I guess I don't care anymore. Thanks for coming."

"I'll meet you back at the office."

"You can go home," she assured him. "I'm okay."

"I'm still waiting for dinner!"

They ended up eating sandwiches and chips from the diner while Sharyn continued through her list of names from the insurance company.

"If you like Dennis for the murders and fires, why finish?" Nick asked while he ate a pickle.

"Because right now, we don't have anything. Like you said, everything is circumstantial. Even if you find talcum and Halon on his gloves, you might be able to find it on twenty other fire fighter's gloves too. Anyone who's been doing the work since 1994. What's the chief's motive in doing all of this? Ernie and Cari went through their lists and couldn't find anyone around here they could tie to it. That includes Dennis."

He understood what she meant. "How many names do you have left?"

"About twelve. I don't know if I expect any of them to be involved. And it wouldn't have to be family. Maybe the chief had a friend who was killed there. That would be hard to look up on the computer."

Nick shrugged. "We could ask him when we find him."

"Ed knows him pretty well." She finished the last of her chips. "Maybe he'd have some ideas."

"I've got the search warrant for the chief's house." Ernie joined them in the office. "I sent Cari home. David is out here. JP's on patrol. Joe is handling a call on his way home. You ready, Nick?"

He nodded and swallowed the last of his Coke. "Let's go."

"Call me if you find anything," Sharyn said as he kissed her cheek. "Be careful."

"Are you going to stay with your aunt tonight?"

"I don't know. I might stay here until we know what happened. I'm not crazy about making Aunt Selma a target."

He touched her cheek. "You be careful too, huh?"

"Always!" She grinned and bit off a piece of her pickle.

"Yeah, right!"

Sharyn returned to her list, determined to get through the names before they found the chief. She already went through the newspaper archives and looked for anything she could find with the Wallace name on it. If the chief was involved with the Clement's building fire, she couldn't find any information on it. He wasn't even working with the fire department in Diamond Springs at the time. He was still a volunteer with the department in Harmony.

The next name on the list caught her attention. *Fred Hays.* Her heart skipped a little. The name was in red, meaning the man died in the fire. She went to the list of victim's names. Fred Hays wasn't there. She went back and checked again.

The newspaper archives carried his obituary. Fred Hays died three weeks *before* the fire. His name was thrown in on the list because he worked for Capitol Insurance before he died. He was survived by his wife, Charlotte, and his daughter, Melinda.

Melinda's father died when they were both in their senior year in high school. Sharyn didn't even realize it. She wasn't close to Melinda. They were more passing acquaintances who smiled at each other in the hallway. In their freshmen year, they shared a locker. After that, they didn't have any classes together again.

She looked up his name and social security number from the spreadsheet. According to the insurance company records, he was fired from Capitol for poor work performance. He was 58. He was with the company for thirty years. Fred Hays was part of a big cutback at the time. He was just another statistic. Within a week of his firing, he died from a massive coronary. Three weeks later, the Diamond Springs office was set on fire and seven other people were dead.

Sharyn dialed the phone with one hand while she looked

in the archive for any sign of Melinda's name being mentioned. "Ernie? I think we might be wrong."

"What's up?"

She explained about Melinda's father. "Melinda has been working as a fire fighter since she got out of high school. That means she worked with Halon. She and her mother were never questioned after the fire according to these records. Maybe there was something in the old records that burned that gave her away."

"But what was her motive, Sheriff?"

"Getting back at the company that caused her father's heart attack."

"It makes more sense that she'd want the place torn down then."

"I haven't connected the dots yet. But the chief may be in danger."

Ed came into the office as she put down the phone. "I can't find Dennis anywhere. No one's seen him. They're making jokes about him running off with that Hays girl."

"What?"

He shrugged. "No one's seen her either. The last time anybody saw the chief, he was with her."

"Come on, Ed. I think it's time to pay a visit to the Clement's building."

"What for? You think the chief might be there?"

"I was thinking about why Monte was killed. We decided it was his connection to the Clement's building. Maybe he saw something he wasn't supposed to see but maybe it didn't have anything to do with the protesters."

"I'll go with you." He got to his feet. "How's your mama?"

"A little shaky but she'll be okay. She's with Selma for the night."

"You're welcome to stay at my place until you get yours settled," he offered with smile as they left the office.

"Thanks, Ed. Until we find out if this was a threat against me, I think I should stay at the office."

"*If?* Don't you think whoever's responsible for all of this was aiming to scare you?"

She explained about Jack Winter being in her house again. "The target was the small den window rather than the bigger one in front. Why would anybody do that?"

He agreed that it didn't make sense. "I don't know. But that's a scary theory."

"Until I know better, I guess I'll stay on the safe side."

They took her Jeep to the Clement's building. Sharyn explained about Melinda on the way. The new fires left the spot looking even worse than before. Scorch marks and pieces of rubble were everywhere. The eerie orange streetlights cast a baleful eye on the old ruin. She wasn't sure what she saw in it as a teenager. Just someplace to hang out that would annoy her father.

Sharyn drew her gun as she got out of the Jeep.

Ed glanced at her and took his out. "Are we worried that she might be here?"

"If Melinda is to blame for what's happened, she's already killed two people now and might be responsible for those lives lost ten years ago. She could even have the chief. I'm not taking any chances."

Their flashlights barely made any headway in the murky basement area beneath the building. They searched thoroughly and couldn't find anything unusual.

"No sign of her," Ed whispered. "Now what?"

"We go up into the building."

"They have it blocked off for a reason, Sheriff. That fire left it unsafe. No one's been up there since. See? The boards are still nailed across the doorway."

Sharyn put down her flashlight and pulled at one. It came off easily in her hand. "We went up here all the time when I was in school. We'll have to be careful."

Ed nodded and glanced around uneasily. He started to go in first but Sharyn went ahead of him. She was so much like her daddy sometimes that it pained him. T. Raymond would've done the same thing. If anybody was going to get hurt, it was him and not his deputies.

The offices were like a maze. The fire department broke through many of the walls while they were fighting the fire. In some places the floors were open to the ground. The girders creaked and groaned as they crept carefully through the darkness. The building felt fragile enough to collapse with a good strong breeze.

Sharyn held her breath as she moved. The air was thick with the smell of smoke. Burned and twisted wires hung down from the ceiling. Doors to offices were open or ripped away. Desks and chairs were where the people left them as they fled in panic from the fire. Women's high heels were pushed off to the side of the hall. Men's sports coats lay mildewing. Rats made nests in paper closets.

"I don't know if we're gonna find anything here, Sheriff." Ed felt the need to convince her to leave. "No one's been up here."

"Someone has." She picked out the footprints on the brown tile with her flashlight beam. "Let's follow those."

Ed nodded, ready to grab something if the building started to fall in on them. "I'm glad I never thought about dating you."

"Besides the obvious reasons," she whispered back, "why's that?"

"Because you're not afraid of anything. It's not healthy."

Sharyn pushed open a door to another office. "Thanks, Ed."

"You're welcome."

She was about to give up. She was going to try one last office. The two floors above them didn't have any access. The only stairway burned, leaving people there to jump or be trapped in the flames and smoke. She pushed open another door to a corner office and stopped walking. "Bingo!"

Ed stopped behind her and peered over her shoulder. "What is it?"

She walked into the room cautiously but there was no sign that anyone was there. The flashlight picked out a room full of memorabilia that seemed to start with yellow newspaper clipping about the fire and end with new ones about the arson attempt at the old courthouse.

Sprinkled between them were pictures of a young girl and her parents. Her father's desk plaque bearing his name, Fred Hays, Executive Vice President. The obituaries for Montgomery Blackburn and Mark Goodson were both taped to a crumbling piece of plasterboard.

Sharyn crouched to light a candle with a match. The office furniture was intact and dusted like someone was about to come back from lunch. Papers dated from that day ten years ago were neatly stacked. A leather chair was clean and still had a colorful cushion on it.

"It's a shrine of some kind." Ed looked around in amazement.

"To her father. She thinks he died because he lost his job here. All this time, all those lives. She didn't want the building torn down because it would ruin everything."

"She had to know it wouldn't stay here forever."

"I don't know if she thinks that way, Ed." Sharyn took out her cell phone but there was no reception in the building.

"She might've killed Dennis." Ed pursed his lips and shook his head. "Maybe he had some idea about what was going on."

"Let's go outside and call around, see if we can find her. You said no one's seen her all day either?"

"That's what they told me."

"Where did they see the chief last?"

"Up on Diamond Mountain. He and Melinda were walking the perimeter set up for the last fire. That was around six last night."

"We know he made it home," she speculated. "Maybe that's why he didn't make it inside."

They met Ernie, Nick and Cari at the office. Sharyn asked Nick if they found anything at the chief's house. "The chief may have a separate pair of gloves he wears for arson and murder. I couldn't test for Halon but there was no talcum powder on his gloves or his clothes."

She told them what they found at the Clement's building. "I think Melinda is our suspect."

"You think she torched the building ten years ago while she was still in school grieving for her daddy?" Ernie couldn't believe it.

"I think it's possible."

"How will we ever get proof on that?" Cari wondered. "That was a long time ago."

"I think we should talk to her mother. She's still alive and living here in the same house. There was something in the original investigation that was done here that Melinda thought gave her away. That has to be why she burned the records and tried to burn the courthouse." Sharyn turned to Ernie. "I'm going to let you take that."

"Okay. I remember she was questioned after the fire. But I don't think I was there to do it." He grinned. "It might've been old Roy Tarnower."

"Thanks, Ernie. I don't want to win the election that way. Call me if you get anything from Melinda's mother."

"What about me, Sheriff?" Cari asked, hoping she wasn't going to be excluded.

"I need an APB put out on Melinda and any vehicles she has registered to her."

"Is that it?"

Sharyn glanced at her watch. "It's late, Cari. You can go home."

"I'd rather look for the Chief and Melinda on the mountain. That's where you're going, isn't it?"

"Yeah. Okay. Put out the APB and let JP and David know what's going on then follow us."

"Thanks, Sheriff."

Sharyn looked at Ed and Nick.

"Don't even think it. I don't know about Nick but I'm going up with you." Ed grinned at her. "And I got a feeling you can't leave Nick down here either."

"We'll take my SUV," Nick decided. "I've got some

shovels and equipment with me in case we get caught up there when the winds turns."

"You just want to show off," Sharyn said with a smile but she put the keys to her Jeep in her pocket.

"If I spent that kind of money on a vehicle, I'd want to show off, too," Ed told her. "Leave the man alone. He's gotta have someplace to stash all those guns!"

The reports from the various fire divisions on the mountain were scattered and sometimes incoherent. They listened to them on the way up the winding dark road. All power was cut to prevent the fire getting any worse. It made driving up there even more hazardous since there was debris in the road.

Slashes of dry lightning lit up the sky. The higher they went, the thicker the smoke got. The fire was contained to the east side of the mountain but a strong breeze could shift it at a moment's notice.

"This is where they were working last night," Nick said, parking the SUV in the road. "The perimeter shifted during the night. But the Chief and Melinda would've been here if they were walking it."

All around them was massive devastation. Trees still stood but they were skeletal charred remains that would never green again. Trenches were dug trying to create firebreaks, tearing down parts of the old forest. Backhoes cleared loose twigs and peat on the ground to try to stop the flames from spreading.

"Let's split up," Sharyn suggested, getting her bearings. "We'll keep an eye out for the chief. But watch out for Melinda. Call if anything looks strange."

Nick and Ed nodded and switched on their flashlights. Nick tucked a small revolver into his pants' pocket.

The face of the mountain was changed forever. Sharyn mourned the land that was so dear to her. Some of her most enjoyable times were spent up here. The trees would grow back in time but the landmarks wouldn't come back. Trees with nicknames, Old Cootie for one, that looked like it had bugs crawling on its trunk. The Twins, two trees that grew together. Even rocks and streambeds were changed because of the dredging. She hiked this area many times but none of it looked familiar.

The acrid smoke caught in her throat. She looked up and saw the red glow getting brighter as she came closer to the area where they were actively fighting the fire.

Ed called her cell phone. "I found the chief. He was tied and gagged and stuffed into an old line shed. It's a miracle he didn't burn up in it. He breathed in some smoke and he's got a big lump on his head but I have an ambulance on the way for him."

"Melinda?"

"That's what he says. He started getting suspicious of her after the courthouse fire. She caught on and knocked him in the head, dragged him here last night. He thought they were going to his place to celebrate."

She nodded. "Okay. Ed. Did you tell Nick yet?"

"Not yet."

"Let him know, please. I'm moving towards the east, I guess. I think I'm walking into the fire line."

"Be careful, Sheriff."

"I will."

She could hear people shouting and the sounds of the county emergency helicopter whirring through the night sky. The heat became oppressive as she got closer. Sparks flitted from the fire to the trees around it. Like tiny bugs they rested and burned through the forest. They were impossible to catch, almost impossible to fight.

"Sheriff!" one of the fire fighters greeted her. It was Bruce Bellows. His face was black with smoke and soot. The firelight etched the weariness on his face. "What brings you up here?"

"I'm looking for Melinda Hays. Have you seen her?"

"She drove up about ten minutes ago when the fire shifted direction again. If you're looking for the chief, she doesn't know where he is. Everyone's been asking."

"I know where he is," she explained without going into detail. "Thanks, Bruce."

That close to the fire, there was no sky. Just a canopy of red and orange light that flared and blotted out the night. Many of the fire fighters had singed eyebrows and lashes from moments when the line of fire shifted abruptly in their direction. The feeling of helplessness was as tangible. Exhausted, bodies aching, they continued to fight what seemed to be inevitable and prayed for rain. Instead they got dry winds and lightning that threatened to start new blazes in other directions.

Sharyn skirted the perimeter of the fire. She put her gun away. There was no way to fire safely. She couldn't tell who was in the trees around her, who was concealed in the smoke.

Lightning snaked across the mountain. Thunder rumbled the old Uwharrie land. Someone yelled out a warning as a gust of wind blew across the main line of the fire. There was a sound of smashing, of trees falling to the earth, as the backhoes tried to create a firebreak. The hot air scorched her face as she tried to get out of the way. Close by her, someone groaned. Excited, terrified voices shouted for everyone to fall back. The firebreak wasn't holding. The fire was out of control.

She started to run back away from the fire when she heard the groan again. She followed it and found someone trapped beneath a fallen tree. She knelt down and tried to get him free. The tree was too big to move by herself. She called for help but she wasn't sure if anyone could hear her over the roar of the fire that was steadily moving closer to them.

"I have to get help," she told the man, wishing she recognized his face. But even her own father would be hard to recognize with a blackened face and singed hair.

"Get out," he screamed. "There's not time."

She glanced around for something to use as a pry lever. "I won't leave you." She found a strong branch and dug it under the tree that trapped his legs. She pushed down hard but it didn't budge.

"What's wrong?" a familiar voice asked.

Sharyn looked at Melinda. "He's trapped. I'm trying to get him out."

Melinda shook her head. "There might not be time."

"We have to try."

Together, they pushed their weight down on the branch. The tree that fell on the fire fighter was old, punky wood. It began to crack rather than move.

"I'll push down," Melinda yelled to her, "you pull him out."

Sharyn nodded and went to take the man's arms. Melinda leaned her weight on the branch and jostled the splintering wood. The fire was jumping from tree to tree above them, surrounding them in its deadly embrace.

Melinda climbed up on the branch and put her whole weight down on it. The tree shredded again. Sharyn fell down as the man's legs were suddenly free.

"Take him back," Melinda shouted at her. "I heard someone else out here."

"I have to take you back too, Melinda," Sharyn told her. "Come with me."

Melinda stared at her. "It was only a matter of time, I suppose."

"Come back with me. We can talk about it."

"I will," Melinda agreed. "But I have to find whoever is out here. Take him back, Sharyn. I'll be there as soon as I can."

Sharyn looked at the inferno that was using up all the oxygen and shriveling the trees. "You can't go back in there. If someone's trapped, he's lost."

"Go on! There's no where for me to escape." She laughed. "Not that I care anymore. They're going to tear it down. I know that. It mattered to me before. It was all I had. Not anymore."

"Melinda, come back with me! You can't do anything out there." A shower of sparks fell on Sharyn's sleeve. It caught fire and burned the material. She hit at it until it was out. The wind whipped flame close enough to make her face feel burned. She turned away from the heat. When she looked back, Melinda was gone.

Hands grabbed at her, pulling her back from the fire. Burning trees toppled around her. She couldn't have followed Melinda. People shouted and dragged the man she and Melinda saved away from the lost area. Sharyn looked at the blaze that followed them towards the road. It snaked closer like it was following a gasoline trail or could sense that they were running from it. They all climbed and shoved into the back of trucks and fled the scene. Before they reached a safe place, the rain started. It was only a sprinkle at first but then it began to pour.

Sharyn lifted her face to it, feeling the cool water like a blessing. It sizzled and cracked in the trees around them as the fire fighters gave a loud cheer.

Epilogue

The elections were over. All that remained was counting the votes. A large group of *Sharyn Howard For Sheriff* supporters were in the ballroom of the Regency Hotel. They were anxiously waiting to hear the news. Don James chewed his fingernails while he kept the phone glued to his ear. Two large TV sets in the ballroom blared out local and state races as they were being counted.

Sharyn moved away from the group of her family and friends. Her face was a little burned but not too painful. The tips of her ears were singed along with some of her eyelashes. She picked up a glass of punch and looked at the multi-colored balloons that were in a net on the ceiling waiting to be dropped.

"Sheriff? This is your party, you know. You could come and say a little something to your friends and supporters." Ernie grinned at her as her eyes focused on him.

"I was thinking about Melinda." She sighed. "There's so much we won't know now."

"I think we know the truth. Her mother knew. I guess she always knew but she was afraid to say it out loud. Melinda thought something was in the records that might give her away."

"We'll never know for sure. That's what bothers me."

"We've got her on everything else. If she wasn't lost in the fire, we'd have her in jail."

"Not for the fire at my house," Sharyn replied. "Not that I believe she did that."

"It's over." Ernie smiled at her. "You have to put it behind you and face the future. You've worked hard to get here. You deserve to be happy about it."

"*If* I win," she argued but she managed to smile at him.

Nick walked up and put his arm around her. "Are we ready for the news? Don says he's on the line with the election officials."

"It's here!" Don yelled. "Sharyn Howard, 82,192 votes. Roy Tarnower, 35,217 votes. Sharyn Howard is elected sheriff of Montgomery County for four more years!"

The balloons dropped and the band struck up a tune. Champagne bottles popped open. People streamed by to congratulate her on their way to the buffet.

"We won!" Ernie shouted. He hugged Nick and Sharyn and did a little dance. "We won!"